The Silent Generation

A Short Lesson in History Anthology

Stephen R. Tracy

64Publications

Though inspired by true events, The Silent Generation is a work of fiction. Because of this, views expressed in the novel are entirely my own, as are whatever factual errors exist in the text. Characters, institutions, and organizations in this novel are works of the writer's imagination. When real, they are used fictitiously without intent to describe their actual conduct.

Author's Note

This is an Anthology of works that I have written and published over the past year and are currently only available as eBooks. As something special, I have taken the time to develop a work such as this one that is in a printed format to reach more audiences and put the pair of eBooks together into a single package. Inside, you will find my two novellas *Grey Two* and *Conspiracy In Action*. Still a part of my *Another Lesson In History* series, *Grey Two* is read more as a soft-sequel to my first full-length novel *The Stone Lotus*, while *Conspiracy In Action* is a soft-*prequel* to my forthcoming second novel to be released sometime next year. Spanning from 1947 to 1963, I hope these tales of Historical Fiction are enjoyed by you all!

Also by
Stephen R. Tracy

Another Lesson in History Series

Book 1: *The Stone Lotus*

1944

The war rages on! With America's left fist, slow advancements are being made to prevent the further genocide in Europe. With its right fist, blows of justice for those lost in Pearl Harbor rain down upon the Japanese. Within a tired and dying world, a race for the future of man has begun. The United States has invested its resources into building atomic arms for large-scale civilian defense. But many are critical of the creation of said weapons… Beyond the reach of government scrutiny and safely out of public view, a top-secret project is being funded by those who are critical of the popular Atom Bomb. Seeking a solution to protect the American people from the inevitable mass destruction the bombs will bring, a group of scientists have invited soldiers and a mysterious student to help find the answer. The clock is ticking. Will they find success, or will the whole plan take an ominous turn within the walls of The Stone Lotus?

Disclaimer

Though inspired by true events, this is a work of fiction. Because of this, views expressed in the novel are entirely my own, as are whatever factual errors exist in the text. Characters, institutions, and organizations in this novel are works of the writer's imagination. When real, they are used fictitiously without intent to describe their actual conduct.

GREY

TWO

01

July 1947
Magdalena, New Mexico

HOT AIR. Hot air and a cloudless sky. His arm dangled from the window of his Chevrolet pickup truck, trying to grab as much of the lingering breeze as he could. The drive down from the Reservation took nearly an hour before he arrived at the corner gas station in the town of Magdalena. Another day of restless ranch folk preparing for the work week ahead made the town come to life. The few cafes here had plenty of foot-traffic in and out as the customers made their way among the grocery and the trading posts. The gas station itself had several cars waiting for open pumps.

Every time he had to make his way into town, Winston Nakai was on edge. The sheer volume of people that always seemed to be active whenever he had the need to run his errands never seemed to dissipate. There were always people. Loud, patience-lacking, masses of people. Maybe to the ordinary man, this was nothing but a slow Tuesday. To Winston, there existed too many wandering eyes and too many loose lips.

The car in front of him pulled away from the gas pump, opening the lane for Winston to pull up. He stepped out of his vehicle awkwardly, having to support himself the entire process. When his right leg swung out of the vehicle, a wooden club clacked onto the pavement. The noise was never something to alarm anyone nearby, but he hated it. No matter the subtlety, it echoed in his ears, reminding him of his tax to the War. He reached across the inside of his vehicle to grab his cane. It was his gift to him from his wife upon returning from Europe. She personally cut it from a Gamble Oak and stenciled meaningful spiritual designs onto it for him. But he still lived in denial of the fact that he will never not need the support to walk. He remembers vividly the moment she gifted it to him, and he hated the sight of it ever since. Not because of its appearance, but because it was to become a part of him. An abnormality.

He popped open the red Chevrolet's fuel cap right as the service kid was running up to the vehicle.

"Regular," is all Winston said to the kid as he limped his way towards the door to the gas station mart. It was not so much a mart, but a place where you could go in and grab yourself a coffee and bakery goods made fresh by the owner and his wife. When he opened the door, the welcome bell rang, and he tried his best to ignore the aroma of all the pastries. All four tables were occupied by people he recognized. A few of them were Indians like himself; ranch owners coming down to socialize the one chance they got every week. At the fourth table sat four teenage boys. All the boys, of course, stopped their laughter and chatter and stared at Winston who clacked his way to the counter. "*It's always the kids that stare*," he thought to himself.

"How are you today, young man?" The clerk asked. He was the owner. An old burly man that appeared to have an issue with most of his customers.

"Peachy," Winston replied. "A pack of Panamas."

"Sure thing."

The clerk reached behind him for the cigarettes just as the service kid came in the door. "Three and forty-eight," he said to the clerk as he went back out to find more work

"Alright, three forty-eight for the gas and another twenty-one cents for the smokes," said the clerk. He slapped the pack of Panamas on the counter and glared at Winston. "Three sixty-nine is your total. Plus, whatever you wanna leave the kid."

Winston pulled out his bill fold and took out four ones. "Change, please."

The clerk scoffed. He took the bills and under his breath Winston heard him grunt, "Injuns".

Just then, a commotion erupted outside. A woman was hollering on the side of the road. Winston did not recognize her. She was older, with curled red hair frizzed out in all directions. Her screaming was relentless, and she was saying something Winston couldn't make out. She kept pointing to the sky with all her fingers.

"Oh damn, she's at it again. Woo-hoo!" The teenage boys at the table were getting riled up. They jumped out of their chairs and made their way outside to listen and chirp at the crazy woman. The clerk dropped the change on the counter for Winston. He collected it all and shuffled his way to the door. The other Indians in the station only stared, not reacting to the commotion outside.

"Move your truck so other patrons can buy some gas," the clerk blurted out right as the door closed behind Winston.

The police had arrived and were trying to talk the woman down. Her clothes were ragged. She was lashing out at the police, tears streaming down her face. She was hysterical. Winston stopped at the door of his car and tried to hear what the woman was saying. None of it was clear, except for a moment when he thought he heard her say, "They got me!". He ducked his way into his Chevy and looked one last time at the scene. The police had pulled her over to their car and were slapping her, trying to get her to calm down. She was snarling, kicking, biting. She looked like an animal. He shook his head, started up his engine, and began making his way back home. God, did he hate coming into this town.

02

July 1947
Alamo Indian Reservation

HE PARKED HIS TRUCK OUTSIDE A SMALL CLAY PUEBLO. The sun was getting low over the hills to the west. The wind was blowing harder up on this flat where he and his family resided, causing the drying clothes on the line to flap violently towards the darkening sky.

He struggled out of his vehicle once again and hobbled towards his dreary-looking home. It was small in scale compared to the houses of those in town. Raising a family of three in a living space where everyone sleeps in the same room only several feet away from where they cook their food. It's difficult on all of them. Especially with his two guests staying there, adapting to an even smaller area took a long time. With a fourth child expected to arrive in a few months' time, he knew he had to talk with his guests.

He pushed open the wooden door to the pueblo. The lock had been broken, fixed, and broken again countless times over the past couple of years. All anyone had to do was just push against the door for it to easily swing open.

"Papa!"

Two young girls came running up to him and hugged his legs. They were both younger than six, but their size was not catching up like it should have. They were small as kids, just like he was small as an adult. It had made his life difficult in the army, being undersized compared to everyone else in his division. He tries not to picture his kids being picked on once they become old enough to participate in grade school.

"Hello, my little *dibés*," said Winston. He smelled the air and looked at two women in the kitchen. They were preparing dinner, cutting chicken parts on the narrow countertop. The entire atmosphere inside the semi-open-air pueblo was still able to capture the scent of a simmering stew. "Do I have time to bring the sheep in before supper, or should I wait?"

"If you hurry now," said the smaller woman. Her hair was long and dark, and her skin was perfectly golden brown. Even with her beauty, she never cared to smile. Winston walked over and hugged her from behind, kissing her on the side of the head. "How was town?" she asked.

"It was busy. As always." He turned back towards the door. He put on his red and black patterned throw as he could feel the air chilling outside with every inch the sun descended. "Where is little Aleshanee?"

"Down for a nap. She missed you today."

Winston gave a half-smile. His kids seemed to be one of the only things that made him happy anymore. The ultimate tragedy in his young life was that he was only twenty-five years old and ready to give up on himself. But as long as his kids were here, he had three reasons to live. Soon to be four. "Have you any sickness today, Ella?" he asked the taller woman. She was white and had her hair pulled back neatly in a bun. She did not smile much either.

"Not today," she said. "I'm feeling much better. Thank you, Winston."

Winston nodded his head. "Is Snake Boy around?"

"I think he's waiting for you down by the corral. He's been out in the field all day."

Winston sighed before pushing through the door.

Down the side of the hill was the valley where his ranch began. A large corral for his sheep herd was plotted next to a much smaller corral with a pair of horses roaming inside. He could see his herd of sheep a few hundred yards away towards the riverbed that separates his land from the neighboring rancher's. Standing down by the corral with his arms crossed on the fencing was the man he was looking for. Maybe not so much a man anymore, but nonetheless a friend.

"Ready to bring them in?" Winston asked while he hopped over the fence of the horse corral.

The friend blinked twice with demon-like eyes that were amber in color. His skin was not that of a human's, but more of a lizard's. He wore a black Stetson hat and a blue long-sleeved plaided shirt and jeans. Hanging loosely from his muscular neck was a black neckerchief, which he used to wipe some grime from his face.

His name was Jacob Desmond. A twenty-three-year-old kid that was one of few surviving victims of a military experiment just two years prior. They turned him from a man into a monster in hopes of creating a new form of human, superior to the rest. He was the product of sadistic visionaries looking to preserve the American race in a time of atomic fear. Now, he is a recluse already at his young age, hiding from the world that surely wouldn't welcome him back. This ranch that belonged to his former wartime bunkmate, Winston Nakai, was pinched into the Indian Reservation in western New Mexico, and was the only place he felt safe. In the two years he's been in hiding since his escape from El Loto de Piedra, nobody has ever come for him. If they hadn't come by now, he believed nobody ever would…

"Hey, Snake Boy!" Winston hollered. He sat atop a horse. It was a brown Morgan named Tapai. "You awake? Let's get this over with before the sun dies."

Jake jumped the fence and hopped on one of Winston's horses; a second brown Morgan, this one named Kai. It once belonged to Winston's mother, whom he did not care to discuss. Kai was a tad underfed, much like the other living creatures on the ranch that were free roaming. The truth, simply put, was that Winston couldn't afford to provide for all on his ranch. They all lived on shy rations. Even animals such as the sheep and chickens struggled to find grass on this side of the hills. The drought had approached its eighth week, and the sheep had eaten away all the green there was in the valley over that time. Nothing was growing fast enough to feed everything.

They circled the small herd of sheep, getting behind the larger part of them and paced the animals into the bigger pen. In all it took thirty-some minutes this night since the herd wasn't all the way to the riverbed. Sometimes getting them away from the embankment is difficult, but thankfully they wouldn't have to bother with that this evening.

Winston dropped the gate of the pen, causing a loud crashing noise that sent bleats out amongst the herd. "Twenty-nine", he counted. All heads accounted for. He looked behind him to Jake who was still on horseback, staring off into the distance as he usually does. "Supper will be ready soon," said Winston. "No time to ride tonight."

Jake swung down off his horse and pulled at the rein towards the smaller pen. He didn't talk as much as he did in the barracks, that Winston remembered. He'd been silent all the last couple years since Jake and Ella found their way to Winston and his family. Winston knew every detail of what happened. He had missed Jake in Europe and was upset at him for some time because his one friend seemingly ditched him right before deployment. But discovering the horrors Jake endured in return was enough for Winston to understand that Jake needed his help. The man was less than human, yet more somehow. He couldn't survive the real world. So young, yet so many years until death would save him. Every night for months, Winston looked at Jake and wondered, *"Why has he not killed himself? He left everyone behind. His family. His friends. What does he live for? Who?"*

Ella. She is who he lives for. The only person from his old world that knows he did not die in the War. Winston understood why Jake left that world. He was from Pheonix, where there are many people. His family wouldn't have been able to protect him. And even if Jake had gone to his parents for help, he would never have been able to breathe fresh air again. Hidden in the corners of his house, complicating the lives of his mother and father. The fewer people that knew he was alive, the easier it was for Jake to cope with permanent seclusion. He brought his girlfriend, Ella, a waitress a little older than Jake, who had a horrible home life and was desperate to build something better somewhere other than Pheonix. Winston did not believe that she cared about Jake's appearance. She was happy with him, even if he was quiet and hated himself. They started their own world adjacent to Winston's. And in truth, made his life a lot easier.

He was the father of three children and had a wife that he found rather bland. He did all the ranch work before Jake came along and before his time in Europe. His wife, Enola, did all the cooking and most of the caring for the kids. The Reservation where they had their ranch was difficult to survive on. Winston's salary for his service in combat had helped pay for a good sum of the family's needs. But that and his disability compensation had abruptly ended several months back for unknown reasons. He could easily have made his way down to the Federal Offices in Albuquerque to straighten that out. But owing to his embarrassment, pride, and hatred for the Feds, he didn't care about receiving the extra money. The drought that was slowly and surely going to begin killing his livestock within the next few weeks didn't push him anymore than it should have. Instead, he believed the rain would come, and that losing a few animals just meant fewer mouths to feed.

The Nakai family and their two long-term guests ate in the very small living area next to the kitchen. There was only the one small table that rested low to the ground, so the two women and children ate first. Jake and Winston stood in the kitchen as always, picking at the prepared food, waiting for the others to finish. The open-air pueblo was catching a comfortable breeze that helped cool them all down after a warm summer evening. It also kept the flies out of the kitchen. The flickering of the lanterns and candles presented a beautiful, dramatic moment in this nightly gathering. Dinnertime here was the only time Jake felt at home. Watching Ella enjoy her prepared meal, playing around with Winston and Enola's young children as if they were her own nieces and nephews. Just like Thanksgivings in Pheonix with his family. He realized his culture and the Indians' were not so different after all, and he waited all day for this nightly routine that seamlessly transported him back to his previous life.

Jake was snacking on some beets, still in the same clothing he had worn out herding. Even his hat was still on, but that was normal. He never took his hat off around anybody, even this family that he was so close to. He had no hair and was ashamed of it.

"Did you get some smokes?" Jake asked.

Winston nodded. "Let's take a walk before the kids get done eating."

———————

The two men sat on the edge of the hill next to the house. The sky was clear, and the stars were sprinkled all over above them. The moon was reflecting a bright glow that allowed them both to see the wide expanse of land around them. The smoke from their cigarettes glided gracefully with the wind away from their faces.

"You know we are grateful that you are here, Jake," Winston started.

Jake did not respond. He continued to stare over the valley.

"You don't have to be withdrawn around us. It's polite to take your hat off when inside."

Jake sighed. "Ella and I appreciate everything you've done for us."

Winston waited for more words, but none came. "Something bothering you today? More than usual, I mean?"

"No. Just living and breathing as we all do."

Winston puffed the cigarette. "Enola and I are worried about the pueblo. The space, at least. Now that Aleshanee is here, and our fourth kid on the way, we're going to need the space where you sleep to put the children in."

Jake bowed his head. "So that's what this is? We overstayed our welcome?"

"I was thinking something more along the lines of... expanding."

"The hell is that supposed to mean?"

"Let's build you two a house of your own on the hill. You

two deserve the privacy and you've helped keep us afloat here. Ella's great with the kids and helping Enola with it all. You've helped more than you know with the animals, and you never stop working as long as there's daylight. We want you to stick around. Use this place as your escape from what you're hiding from."

"Thank you." Jake inhaled smoke. "Sorry, I didn't intend to come off so hot. I'm indebted to you forever, you know that?"

"Pssh. No, you're not."

"Without you, I'd be nowhere. I owe you my life."

Winston shook his head. "Just…be here with us. Raise my kids as if they were your own. Protect this land with the same belief. That's my only expectation."

A moment passed, then someone came up behind them. "The kids are all done." It was Ella.

The men finished off the stick and got up. Winston made his way to the pueblo. Jake stood facing Ella. She had a smile as she looked into his eyes. Red, golden eyes that didn't show any emotion. Gemstones that were priceless in the man she loved. She gave him a hug, feeling the bulkiness of his body. The rough, scaley skin that covered every inch of him. She laid a kiss on his cheek. It still bothered her when she felt the pebbly flesh against her lips. Slowly, she was getting used to it. They held each other close.

"Do you know how much I miss seeing you throughout the day?" She asked him. Her hair was all the way down and flowing in the wind. Her eyes were green during the daytime, but when the moonlight was hitting them tonight, they became dark silvery mirrors that reflected onto Jake, reminding him who he really was deep down. He only smiled at her without saying anything. "A whole lot," she said. "I wish you'd come and spend more time inside with me. It's a lot cooler in the pueblo."

"The heat doesn't bother me," Jake said.

"Couldn't you just come up and say 'hello' once or twice? Check on me?"

"There's a lot of work to be done. I have to make up for all the work Winston can't do."

She sighed. "When can we raise a kid of our own? You'd be a good father—"

"No. No. You know how I feel about that."

"But don't you want a purpose in life?"

"My purpose is here, with you."

"That's fine and all but, I know you want more."

"We don't know what would come of the kid. It could come out horribly deformed. In great pain. I don't want to be responsible for ruining its life. He'd have a father that looks nothing like the other kids' fathers. It's too limited of an environment to raise a child here. It's not something I could burden my child with to look up and see...*this*." He examined himself.

Jake was silent. His face was blank again.

"All I'm saying is," Ella continued, "you have a soft side to you. Behind that shell, is the man I love. I will never leave you for whatever reason. I'll be here for you. But you're more ambitious than you try to admit. Please, think about it. That's all I ask."

He nodded subtlety, hugged her once more, then walked at her side back to the pueblo.

03

July 1947

Alamo Indian Reservation

HIS THROAT BEGAN TO CLOSE. Or so it felt. Jake shot up from his slumber, struggling to find his breath. Panting and coughing to remember how to breathe. Ella woke up next to him and attempted to calm him down, talking low and rubbing his back, doing whatever she could to help him. Their bed was only layers of rugs, throws, and blankets very low to the floor situated around the corner from where Winston and his family slept. Jake's struggle to breathe was a weekly occurrence. It would wake most of the pueblo whenever his attacks happened. Thankfully, over the past year, it became a less common occurrence. Ella and Winston both agreed that it is some form of traumatic fatigue he experiences that causes him to spasm when his nightmares trigger something inside him. Jake was familiar with this scenario. He would wake up unexpectedly back inside El Loto when his cellmate, Cesar, would have nightmares. He'd often wake up screaming or flailing out of bed as nonsense leapt off his tongue.

Now, Jake struggles with the same nodus. Ever since he had miraculously escaped the facility he expected to die in, he rarely enjoyed a peaceful sleep. He'd see the needles, the faces of the scientists, The Pit, and his two friends that he would never see again outside of his dreams: Henry Winslow and Cesar Martinez. Without a doubt, he believed Cesar was killed or captured at some point after their escape. He was tortured badly at El Loto and driven to madness much faster than the others. He was a lot smarter than Jake was, younger as well. He had no cause to be placed at El Loto. At least, that's what he and Henry believed. Jake and Henry were there by choice. A regretful decision they each had made. And it cost Jake nearly everything.

He still remembers the day he and Henry parted ways, back on the night of Christmas (though neither of them knew the day, a vestige of delusion), almost two years ago. They were hiding out in a railyard after a long day of running. Jake was set on his plan to find Winston Nakai, praying that he was alive and could offer sanctuary. But he couldn't convince Henry to come with him. After all they had been through together. Their appearances altered to a hideous state. It didn't matter to Henry as much. He wanted to be home with his mother in Chicago. Nothing Jake could say was going to tear Henry away from her.

And that's where they left each other. Henry hopped on a freight headed east and Jake traveled on foot to the town of Magdalena, where he used a payphone to call Ella. He was starved and exhausted from all his travels. Jake hid in the town for days, eating scraps left behind the diner, going through resident's trash cans, stealing milk off their porches. A week went by, then Ella arrived on a bus with a small bit of luggage. She was horrified at the first sight of Jake, but her shock evaporated quickly as they first embraced each other. She had thought he was dead after the letters stopped coming sometime around his scheduled deployment. Then hearing from Jake's parents that they received the telegram informing of his death confirmed her suspicion. It hurt her more than Jake thought it would, and it made him love her more. After a few days, she was able to find the Nakai ranch through interactions in Magdalena. A neighboring rancher was able to point her the way.

Winston was not at the pueblo for the first month, however.

He was still in Europe dealing with his injury. It was extremely difficult for Ella to persuade this woman, Enola Nakai, to allow her and the mutant Jake to stay with them. Jake pleaded with Enola and swore that he knew Winston from the Army. Jake offered to do all the ranch work, and Ella would provide additional help where it was needed in the absence of her husband. The Nakai children, only two of them at the time with the third child due in a few months, lacked proper nutrition. Enola could not raise them herself. And she was very soon grateful that these two angels arrived when they did.

Jake rolled himself out of bed and quietly said to Ella that he was going for a walk to clear his head. He threw on a flannel, his hat, and some pants, then walked barefoot out the front door. The Earth crunched beneath his hardened feet as he made his way down the hill towards the corrals. The night air would be comfortable to most, but he could feel no difference in the change of temperature. Only if it were extremely cold could he feel any difference in the climate. And it had been a long while since he last felt any sort of chill. It was one of the very few things he didn't hate about his condition; he never had the need to dress according to the weather.

So, whenever he had his midnight attacks, he'd sit on the edge of the wooden fencing that penned the horses. The breeze was catching his flannel, flapping behind him, but he couldn't feel the sensation of the cloth brushing his skin. He was still accustomed and thought it more respectful to have some sort of garments on so long as he left the house, even if they were unnecessary to him.

The horses in the pen avoided him at night. Jake's eyes, when light would catch them at certain angles, would reflect orange, sort of like a nocturnal predator's. The flashing glow would be unsettling for the horses, and they'd keep their distance. The sheep in the other holding area were making an inordinate amount of noise, bleating and bah-ing like a coyote had entered the pen. Jake went over to investigate. He didn't bring out his firearm tonight which was probably unwise, but he wasn't scared of a coyote or two.

He looked at the group and saw that all the sheep were still standing and making more noise now that they saw his eyes. He did a head count quickly and was forced to count again. And again.

Twenty-eight sheep.

He counted three times, and it was twenty-eight every time. One short. He and Winston each counted twenty-nine just when they brought them all in. Now, Jake was convinced something had gotten into the pen and pulled out one of the sheep. The fence was intact all around. The gate was closed and bolted. He couldn't picture how one could have escaped.

Then he heard it: a deep, bleating and crying sound somewhere in the direction of the creek. He walked cautiously out into the dark field, trying not to make much of a sound with his feet so he could triangulate the noise. He was getting closer, but the noises from the lone sheep were becoming fewer. He'd walked nearly fifty yards when he could make out the silhouette of the sheep on the ground. He rushed ahead and was darting his eyes around looking for any predators. The coast seemed clear, so he knelt next to the sheep that was breathing heavily and wheezing. Jake put his hands over the animal, panicking it at first, but quickly calming itself as Jake checked for injuries.

Its legs were broken. The front two, at least. Jake stood up and put his hands on his hips. It was exhausted and dirty, too.

There was no blood, no bite marks, and just a few scratches on its legs. It looked as if it had fallen off the roof of a house. Jake looked around at the open field in dismay, then back to the pained creature on the ground. *"What could have gotten this thing that far up in the air?"*

He bent over and grabbed the sheep by its haunches and began carefully pulling it back towards the corral, trying not to injure the animal any further. It wasn't putting up a fight, and it weighed nothing to Jake as he hauled it through the desert. The sound of the other animals grew louder as he drew closer to the pen. *"There isn't a bird big enough to pick this thing up. Nothing out here is big enough to toss it up into the air where its legs would break. And it was all alone? Left for dead!"*

Jake was already bewildered at this incident in the night, and it only became worse moments later. In the distance, the echoing drum of canons disrupted the night. At least, that's what it sounded like to Jake. Several large booming noises sent a jolt through his body. Appearing above him immediately after was a bright orange wave shooting across the sky like a car-sized meteor crashing down. It was headed in the direction of the canyons to the north but made no sound in its travels. Just a noiseless fireball that glided into the horizon. Then, just as it passed over the hills, a flashing light and a distant explosion erupted.

Jake's eyes became wide, and he dropped the sheep's legs where he was standing, sprinting past the corral and up the hill to the pueblo.

04

July 1947
Alamo Indian Reservation

"WINSTON! WAKE UP! A PLANE WAS JUST SHOT DOWN! CLOSE TO THE CANYONS!"

The entire pueblo awoke. The infant began to scream.

"I didn't hear anything," Winston said with an annoyed tone.

"There were shots fired somewhere to the south," said Jake. "Sounded like heavy artillery. We gotta go see the crash!"

Winston groaned. "Why?"

"Could be a foreign plane. It's probably still on the Reservation."

Winston didn't say anything. Enola was up and cradling the screaming child. Ella was sitting up and rubbing her eyes.

"I'm going," Jake continued. "I'm curious to see what it's all about. It's not far from here and whatever business is going on, could end up involving us." He turned and hurried his way out the door, awkwardly shoving his feet into some boots without stopping.

"Wait, Jake!" Winston hollered.

"You're going?" Enola asked.

"It's not safe to ride alone at this hour. And if he's right about how close it is to the ranch, we must see what all is going on. We'll observe from a distance." He got out of bed and threw on a dirty coat, some boots, then grabbed his lever-action Winchester rifle and his cane.

"Please be careful!" Enola yelled to Winston.

Behind him, the screaming of his youngest child was lost in the breeze and flapping of clothes drying on the line. The wind had picked up remarkably since the family went to bed. He looked down to the corral where Jake was already departing on Kai's back, pushing an incredible pace to the canyons north of the ranch. Just as Jake had said, it looked much like a plane crash. The light pulsing over the hills looked like a smaller setting sun on the horizon line. Now, his interest had piqued, and he started hustling towards the corral.

Jake was well ahead of Winston. His urgency was intense as he encouraged his horse to navigate the canyon's crevices. The walls were fifty feet high on both sides, and the moonlight was not lighting a path as well as he'd hoped. However, the horse beneath him was gliding with grace through the passageways, not concerned of the time of day with its far superior night vision. It was exciting for Jake. Nothing has happened for nearly two years since he began living on the ranch. Now, a major event was unfolding less than a mile from him.

His thoughts raced. Whatever was shot down, was done so promptly. A restricted aircraft? One of Japanese or German origination, perhaps? That could be the beginning of something much larger in scale. But it made no sound as it flew over him! Was it his own shock that misguided his ears? No. He could hear the animals clearly. Whatever it was, he had to approach with caution since this was surely going to bring some attention to the area. Plus, he was unarmed.

The walls of the canyon began to lower as the path widened. Ahead, he believed to see sloped terrain where he directed his mount. He just needed to see how much farther he had to go. The glow was much lower now, and he had to hurry if he wanted to inspect from a distance. At least, at first.

The ground beneath him began to angle upward towards the canyon flats. It wasn't long before he was at the top. The brush was dry and heavy, and his horse was struggling to find its way through. Jake calmed the horse down as it was wanting to lift off the ground to avoid the scraping of the brush. He hopped off the animal and tied the reigns to one of the stems of a dried-out bush.

Jake crept forward through the thickets, winding his way through like the cold-blooded reptile he resembled. He ignored the twigs and sticks around as they were easily shrugged off by his unique flesh. Keeping his head low, he approached the edge of the plateau. He looked onto a wide expanse of flat range that must have marked the end of the reservation. He drew this conclusion from the amount of cattle and obsolete farm equipment resting on the near side of the valley just below the sloped cliff he was on. And beyond that, the plane wreck.

Jake was staring at a dozen human-sized embers burning atop sections of the destroyed plane, right in the middle of the two-hundred-acre valley. It was less than five minutes on foot if he were to get down there to investigate. Surely, the pilot had died. Anybody would have when colliding with Earth at hundreds of miles an hour. Once Winston was able to catch up with him, they would have to go together to confirm the origin of the plane.

He could hear Winston's horse coming through the canyon behind him, the echoes spiraling up the walls. Jake whistled a signal as best he could with his fingers to grab Winston's attention. Not long after, he heard the horse scaling the slope behind him. But Jake saw something coming from the left side of the valley, so he did not turn to welcome Winston over.

A light flickered on and was advancing towards the crash.

The sound of a rusted-out muffler sputtered and shrieked through the valley.

"Joe Foreman," Winston said, pushing away the brush with his cane. He crouched beside Jake and said, "He's an old guy. Sells and breeds cattle off his land, here."

"You know him well?" Jake asked.

Winston shrugged. "Doesn't like being this close to the Reservation. Not too many friends in town that I recall, either." They watched as the truck approached the flames.

"Why don't I hear any sirens? Surely, someone had to have reported this."

Winston shook his head very slowly as he beheld the sight. It was all too familiar to him. A burning wreck of an aircraft that smoldered in the distance. The smell of fuel burning and smoke rising. It made his nerves stand on end, waiting for the sound of something near and awful. He held his breath as he watched Joe Foreman's truck come to a stop at the edge of the crash. It appeared the size of a toy car from where they were perched.

Joe Foreman stepped out of his green Chevrolet pickup truck. He braced his hand on the top of the cab as he reached between his seats for the Winchester Model 1912 shotgun that he carried with him whenever he left his house. Surrounded by Indians, he would protect himself and his land at all costs.

He was tired, crabby, and excited when he heard something crash into his cattle lands. He was still wearing his long underwear and had only thrown on his dirty cargo boots to get him out the door. Sixty-seven years of age wasn't slowing him down from doing his own investigating tonight. He was never in a war, but talked patriotically as if he gave every limb on his body to his country. Wartime was a nostalgic feeling for him, oddly enough. The image of the Great American War Machine was embedded in the temporal lobe of his brain. He lived for the Stars and Stripes.

Foreman moved cautiously past the first pillar of crackling fuselage. His face was pursed into a red wrinkled tangle with grey beard hairs flailing about in the wind. His finger rested on the trigger, and he kept the stock buried into his shoulder as he advanced. The air around him was hot and causing sweat to dribble into his eyes. He ignored the burn. The further into the crash site he went, the more the heat radiated, and the more the air smelled like wet paint.

He heard a pounding sound, as if a heavy door was being beaten on somewhere near him. Just to his right, he saw a dome of dark glass attached to a part of the fuselage. That's where he heard the pounding. A repetitious *thud thud thud*. It was the cockpit. He hurried over, assuming that the pilot was stuck inside. A bit of flame was burning just behind the cockpit. He looked around at the bits of twisted metal and could not identify any symbols anywhere. If it was a foreign fighter, had best be prepared.

He reached the black dome and tapped the glass with the barrel of the gun. The thudding stopped. "Hey!" He yelled. "What country you from!" Tapped a couple more times. "Are you American? Or you one of those oriental fellers?"

Nothing.

He studied the glass and looked to see if anything was keeping it from opening. He saw that the cockpit's seal was dented at the base of the glass. It was an odd-looking plane now that he was getting a closer look. There were no parts that were angular or pointed. All the burning wreckage was covered in ash and, in parts, melted already. But anyone that had an observational eye could see that the plane was entirely made up of flat, smooth parts.

"I see you're stuck!" He yelled again, "Ima break you outta there! Cover your eyes!"

He stepped back and wound up the butt of his gun to strike near the seal. Then, before he could bring his momentum forward, the dome shot straight out at him, blasting him in the upper body and chin. It hit him with the hollow smack of a cannonball, and Joe Foreman was sent flying onto his back ten yards away beside a pile of charred plane parts. His gun rested between him and the now-open cockpit. But Joe Foreman laid very still. Unconscious.

Up above the canyon, they couldn't see what happened clearly. They saw some shadows fly around for a moment, followed by a soft "*bang*".

"I don't like the looks of this," Jake said. "I think we gotta go and see what's happening."

"I'm with you," said Winston. "You armed?"

"No. Forgot to bring one with me. Got caught up in the action."

"Take my rifle down. I'll be behind you. It's going to take a minute for me to get down this hill and over the fence."

Jake nodded. He stood up and ran over to Winston's horse to take the rifle off the saddle strap. He checked the clip to see only three bullets loaded. He couldn't think of a reason to need any more than that. He made his way over to the side of the hill and saw Winston part way down already, easing his way on his buttocks and using the cane for support. His physical actions made him appear forty-years older than he was. It upset Jake having to watch his friend struggle with such a handicap. With the front of that foot of his taken from him in the war, being a rancher as young as he is, would be impossible if Jake weren't around to help.

Jake slung the rifle over his shoulder and descended towards the fence at the base of the hill. It was only a minute later when he passed Winston, who was swearing at himself, frustrated he couldn't move swiftly. Jake decided it was best not to say anything to further discourage him. Soon, Jake was at the base of the hill and standing against the wire fence that marked the beginning of the Foreman ranch, or more likely, the beginning of the Reservation. It was chest-high, and the top wire was barbed, yet Jake ignored this detail. He needed to get to the crash without any further delay. He gripped the barbed fence with his hands, and without feeling as much as a prick, pushed the fencing down in front of him. It collapsed under his weight with hardly any resistance. He stepped over the wiring and flattened it down to make it so Winston could pass through. It was one of the few gifts that mad scientist, Robert Gatta, left him with. His skin was much stronger and different from that of a normal human's. Jake couldn't remember the last time anything pained him since his escape.

He maneuvered through the farm junk towards the dying flames. A build-up of old trailers, cattle guards, and large piles of wooden pallets lay scattered all over the ground. Perhaps this was Foreman's way of constructing another barrier between himself and the Indians. Mounds of steel and rust that laid without a purpose on only this side of his land. Once through the clutter, Jake ran among a few cows that were starting to make their way towards the river, giving him a straight path to the crash. It was much harder to see now as the moon was hidden behind some clouds. The last bits of dancing flames were all the light being given. He pulled the rifle around and ran with it in his right hand, then pulled his bandana-style neckerchief over his nose.

05

July 1947

Alamo Indian Reservation

JAKE CONFIDENTLY STRODE THROUGH THE PILES OF DESTROYED AIRCRAFT. The flames were no longer burning, and it became very difficult to see anything through the veil of smoke and dusk. At every significantly-sized piece of fuselage, he paused to scan for any symbols and markings. Nothing revealed its origin. It was plain silver in color. Or at least it had been before all the paint was burned off.

Then he saw the old man flat on his back. He was lying next to a large black bowl that was certainly the cover of the cockpit. It must have ejected from the aircraft and struck him badly. That's when Jake heard someone speaking across from the body of Joe Foreman. Jake readied his rifle and slowly walked over to what looked like the uncovered cockpit. Each step he took was carefully placed back on the ground to avoid making too much noise.

He heard the talking again. It wasn't English being spoken.

Jake pulled the hammer back and cocked the lever, loading a bullet into the chamber. He approached the voice, ready to fire. His hands were steady, and he was prepared to do what he must to whatever enemy sat behind the controls.

What he saw was something he couldn't at first comprehend.

Sitting behind the control panel to the plane was a bleeding figure that was smaller than the average man. It looked about the size of a young high school kid. It was wearing a black and orange jumpsuit with a unique symbol over where its heart should be. Silver wings. A black helmet rested in its lap, but it had an odd shape to it. The bleeding was coming from the lower abdomen where a tear in the suit could be observed. A lot of blood. Dark red in color, just like a human's. What wasn't human, or entirely human, was the face and head of the being. It could fool the eye from a distance. But from just a few feet away, it was clearly different. The cranium was stretched back abnormally. Just a tad bigger than a human skull but shaped like an oval if seen from the side. The eyes were small and dark. The mouth appeared to be lacking lips. The nose was so small, it didn't protrude from the face. It looked just like two holes punched above the mouth. And the pigment of skin was sickly. Grey. The darkness around him surely was playing tricks on his eyes.

A bit of blood trickled from the mouth of the creature. It blinked, proving it was still alive. Jake's eyes were strained open. He didn't know whether to fire to end its pain, or whether to try to ask it something. The being made his decision for him.

It spoke. It sounded human when it talked, wheezing out words that sounded like nothing Jake had ever heard before. Like an ancient language that was lost until now.

"What the hell are you?" Jake said, breathing his thoughts out loud.

The creature moved its head forward and examined Jake, looking him in his eyes and admiring the facial features that *also* resembled something nonhuman. The creature was talking again. It sounded confused as it looked at Jake.

"I don't know what you're saying," said Jake.

Just then, Winston came up behind Jake. "Where's he from?" He must not have seen the being yet.

Jake paused. "Not a 'he'."

"What?" Then Winston saw it. His jaw dropped.

The being went to reach for something beside itself, and it raised the object slowly at Winston. Not at Jake. It had already lost so much blood; it didn't have the ability to raise whatever it was quickly or high enough. It looked sort of like a handgun.

"Jesus!" Winston yelled as he tripped over himself trying to evade.

Jake shot once into the chest of the creature, and the gun fell out of its hand. Five fingers, like a human. The body went limp. He lowered the gun and stared for a moment while Winston scrambled his way back up to his feet.

"It was going to shoot me!" Winston hollered. "What even is that thing? That's not a person, is it?"

"No." Jake was in awe at the sight of the body. "It's not. I don't know what it is, but it seemed to think the same when it looked at me."

Winston looked at Foreman's body on the ground behind him, then went over to determine his condition.

"It spoke to me in a weird language," Jake continued. "It was trying to tell us something." He got up closer to the creature and looked at all the controls. Everything was dark inside, but the number of switches and dials and buttons was overwhelming to Jake. "This is one odd plane, Windy." Windy was the nickname Jake had given Winston at basecamp when they met. Back then, Winston was the fastest man in the unit. Jake felt the nickname was fitting and self-explanatory for someone that had such speed. Now, of course after his losing a foot, the name seemed ironic.

"Foreman's alive!" Winston said to Jake. "He's got a dent in his chin, and he bit his tongue clear off. Looks like some teeth are missing, too. But he's alive."

"What should we do?"

"We must get him help. You carry him back to the horses and we'll get him to the pueblo."

"What about this thing? We can't leave it here in the middle of his field."

A roar of engines rose behind them, back towards the Foreman house. A stream of lights bounced up and down all around them. The search party had finally arrived.

"Authorities!" Winston yelled. "We gotta get you out of here!"

Jake looked at the lights. His eyes flashing and reflecting them, much like a cat's. He looked down at the unique corpse. Swearing under his breath, he began to run back towards the canyon.

"Hey! What about Foreman?"

"They'll take care of him!" Jake yelled as he continued his sprint.

"Shit." Winston shook his head, and using all his energy, he began striding behind Jake as best he could.

Jake helped push Winston back up the steep hill to the plateau where their horses waited. Once at the top, they turned around to see a dozen vehicles surrounding the crash site. All were dark in color. From the looks of it, they were Dodge Staffs; military vehicles. Their lights flooded the area. A couple of local police cars joined the scene a few minutes behind.

Crouched in the bushes, the friends watched the operation unfold.

06

July 1947

Alamo Indian Reservation

THE COUPLE DOZEN MEN THAT WERE RUMMAGING AND SORTING THROUGH THE WRECKAGE HAD JUST FINISHED UP WITH WHATEVER THEY CAME HERE TO DO. It took an hour of coordinated and organized dealings that looked to have been rehearsed a hundred times over. And they were dressed for the occasion: matching green Army uniforms.

Jake and Winston sat quietly on the edge of the canyon flat, crouching behind the dried-out vegetation. Neither of them spoke more than a couple words here and there as they tried to keep themselves awake for the entire show. Though it was dark, they tried to be as still as the tiny cacti surrounding them while the operation was being executed.

What they had been able to see, thanks to the many floodlights and headlights circling the plane parts, was a lot of constant motion. Nobody stopped moving. The second they all had arrived, the job they came to do was already in action. The only people that were not working, and appeared to be chatting through all of it, were the couple of local policemen that were talking to one of the Army men. The policemen were never allowed past the perimeter of the crash. Anytime one of them attempted to move forward or sneak a peek, the Army man talking to them would obstruct their path and view as best he could. Flashes of white light popped at different spots of the crash; photos were being taken first. Four large green trucks with long trailers attached rumbled onto the scene, sending the men immediately into a frenzy of moving parts of the plane onto the trailer beds. As soon as one trailer was full, a tarp was thrown over the cargo and tied down with straps. The truck would then leave right after. Efficiently, it was all taken away. The parts of the plane were so small, the biggest piece only needed six men to lift it.

The policemen had left. A handful of green Staffs followed. Only one truck with a trailer sat waiting with a few other Army cars. This was when Jake and Winston sat up with curiosity.

Two bodies were lying flat on the ground: Joe Foreman, and the oddity. Foreman was placed onto a gurney while pictures were being snapped. Hand gestures were dramatically thrown around. Until the farmer awoke.

Soon, he was being supported by a couple of the men. They must not have known all that was wrong with him yet, but they didn't want him standing. They repeatedly had their hands held up, palms out, telling him to take it easy, probably. But Foreman was stubborn. He attempted to stand on his own and collapsed to his knees in doing so. That's when he submitted to the officials and they walked him over to one of the cars, helped him in, and drove him back in the direction of his house.

While that was going on, a white body bag was deployed to shroud the different being. More photos were taken, and it was lifted onto the back of the trailer, sent on a ride, likely to the nearest government facility. Some more of the Dodges left with it, escorting it back to the road.

A few men still were down at the now-stripped sight. The lighting was much lower currently, and the first pink rays of the sunrise could be admired rising over the hills. One man was bent down on a knee, looking at something very closely, while the other two men were shining flashlights onto whatever he was looking at. The one man stood up and did something that turned the two spectators white:

He began walking towards them!

His attention was mostly focused on the ground while one of the other men's flashlights shined a path. The other was shining the light up to the tops of the canyon. They were following footprints.

Winston fell backwards clumsily as his heart pounded against his chest. Jake turned back, staying as low as possible, moving through the brush. He pushed Winston upright and forward towards the horses.

"Stay low and quiet," Jake whispered. "But move faster."

"Do we leave the animals?" Winston asked.

"God no. We gotta get them out of here, too."

They made their way a hundred feet to their horses. Jake looked back and didn't see any lights shining. He helped Winston up onto his horse, Taipa, and sent him on his way. Carefully and quietly, he picked his way down into the canyon with Winston's guidance. Jake hopped up on his ride and still couldn't see or hear anything. He pulled his reigns around and directed his horse to follow Winston. The horse placed its hooves onto the downward slope and meticulously found its way down to the canyon floor. If Jake had been calm, he would not have panicked and botched his actions in this moment: he kicked at the side of his horse to get it to move faster, but this resulted in giving Jake away to the pursuers.

The horse let out a whinny, just loud enough to send an echo off the canyon walls.

Jake clenched his teeth as his horse galloped quickly though the canyon. He knew what he had done and regretted it instantly. He almost wanted to cry when the yellow glow of a flashlight hit the canyon wall just to his left. He came around a curve and entered the narrow part of the path where his horse effortlessly strode though. He kept replaying his fault in his head. His adrenaline had controlled him, and he kicked his horse. It was going to move fast enough regardless! "*Why the hell would I do that?*" He kept cursing himself as he rode. His curiosity put him in this position, and he just couldn't leave it alone. He *had* to see the plane crash? No, he didn't. What he did was endanger himself. Ella. The Nakai's. The people that were behind him knew somebody was there watching them. "*The stupid footprints! If we hadn't gone down there to the crash, they wouldn't have known we were watching!*"

He saw Winston ahead of him as they reentered the Nakai valley. The walls on either side abruptly ended, sort of like a formal exit from the canyon. The earth crunched beneath his horse's hooves here in the valley. Everything was as dead as Jake surely was going to be. He knew this wasn't over with.

"I'm sorry. I…I wasn't thinking."

"It won't be difficult for them to know where to look now, will it?"

Winston and Jake were in a small, covered horse stable. It was a shelter they had poorly built for the horses when it was storming. It was less of a stable and more of a covered corral. The daylight was beginning. The early morning rooster crows could be heard around the ranch. Dried out, starving, pathetic rasping *cuckoos*. They were hiding their horses here in the stable for now, while they went over the details.

Winston was furious at Jake. "They'll be coming here," he said to him. "You couldn't just let me sleep. You had to come in, pull me away from my family, and out into danger. I was happy where I was. Now, who knows if I'll ever see them again. This is the kind of *shit* that gets you in trouble, Jake! Always! Especially when the government comes to the Reservation. Too much friction. It's never diplomatic when feds come to these lands."

"I know. I'm sorry. You have no idea how sorry—"

"Sorry means nothing, Snake Boy. What we must do is plan for these men to arrive at our front step. I'm guessing they'll start going door-to-door on the Reservation, starting by us here in the north. Dammit!" He yelled, slamming his cane against the side of the stable. "I want nothing to do with the Army anymore, Jake. We just invited them here by going out there. They'll put the pieces together, see two different footprints, know two different people. And most us Indians don't have horses, so they'll be looking to the ranches first if they see their tracks. This will be an open and shut investigation for them, dammit!" He slammed his cane against the wall again. "What even was that person inside the plane? Maybe another human experiment, like you?"

"It didn't look like any human I've ever seen. Certainly, like nothing from El Loto."

"Did you get a good look at it?"

"Sort of. I mean, the shape of the head was different. And whatever it was, was smaller than the average man *or* woman."

"*Shit*. It doesn't matter, I suppose. It's gone and dead, now. Probably was a Japanese spy that was badly mutilated after the crash. They're smaller people. That makes the most sense. But we need to prepare for those officials that are going to be combing over our land."

"I really don't think that was a human, Winston—"

"Shhh. I don't want to know what it is, Jake. I need to focus on what's important now: keeping our kin safe."

"Okay," Jake took a deep breath. "Whatever happens, I

promise you, I will do anything to protect you and your family. I need a second to think."

"We don't have time to think, Jake. They'll be here sooner than you know. And what could you do for us? You're hiding from these people. For all any of us know, you're a fugitive. You get discovered; we all go down. You can't show your face around here."

Jake bowed his head. He removed his hat, revealing the hairless, snakeskin scalp. "What do you suggest?"

Winston looked to the sky and closed his eyes. Taking deep breaths, he weighed his options. Only one thing came to mind that could help them out of this mess. And the thought of it made him sick.

He looked at Jake, who was visibly fighting tears. He gripped Jake's shoulder and told him, "This is how we're going to do it…"

07

July 1947
Alamo Indian Reservation

WINSTON WAITED NERVOUSLY AT THE SIDE OF HIS PUEBLO. He was already on his fifth cigarette in the past hour, attempting to calm his nerves as best he could. He was rested up against the clay house, staring straight out into his valley towards the river. The heat of the July morning was beginning to intensify, which made his composure waver with each passing minute. His palms were sweating. The nerves in his hands were shuttering, and his breath was shaking. He continued to suck down his cigarette just so he could begin on another. How he wished he had some sort of alcohol to dull his thoughts right now. It had been so long that he'd been seated here on the hard ground, going over every scenario in his head that could possibly be brought upon him. His rear had begun to ache, which caused him to shift uncomfortably more and more as he waited. His family was inside. They were not to talk; pretend that English was unspeakable for them if they were asked anything by the coming officials. Winston worried about the kids. It made his stomach crawl thinking that they could be put on the spot. They were too young to understand what was going on.

"Don't stop until the river widens," Winston said to himself under his breath. The growling of engines could be heard as vehicles charged up the dirt road from the south, up towards the pueblo.

Ella was sitting on the river's embankment, tears falling from her face. Jake had finally disappeared around a slight bend in the river. She could only pray and wait for his timely return. She kept peeking carefully over the edge of the embankment back towards the pueblo hill, her eyes straining to make out any visitors in the area. None could be seen.

She looked towards the canyons in the north, where earlier that morning Jake had explained to her all that transpired. The different shades of dullish brown landscape surrounded her. Even on the edge of the riverbed, everything was near death. Gloomy, desert-like lands that were vacant of thriving life. That was the Reservation, in her eyes. Depressing as that is, it was better than where she had grown up. The abusive homelife in the city that she escaped was still hellish compared to the simple, impoverished life amongst the Indians. And with Jake here with her, it was made much, much better. Looking past the unfortunate physical features he was cursed to live with forever, she loved him more for his resilience and fight to come out of that experiment alive. And to first think of adding only *her* back into his life, leaving behind his family and friends, she knew she wanted to be with him here in the middle of nowhere.

Caught with her mind wandering in this anxiety-induced daydream, she was forced to throw herself quickly backwards, panicking at the sight of what was coming from the main entrance of the canyon.

Jake walked in the river with a rope slung over his shoulder.

Words kept flowing from his lips, drowned out by the gurgling current around him. The water was much lower than it should have been at this point. Though it was nearly six feet deep here, it was nonetheless several feet lower than it normally should have been at this time of year. Around the bend, about a mile or so from Winston's land, more inlets of flowing water entered the main channel where he now walked. Some inlets ran low, and others not at all.

He was apologizing. Not to anyone near him, but to the people he had endangered with his mistakes. Water was pushing up towards his scaly neck as he said the names of all those people repeatedly. Even the names "Henry" and "Cesar" had been spoken once or twice throughout his trek. Traumatized by the thought of putting the people he loved in the path of danger terrified him. More so, what would they do with *him*? "*The government would love to get a hold of me, test on me, pull me apart to see what I could be made useful for,*" he thought. Apologizing to no ear near, he felt guilty as it was for believing he never did enough at El Loto de Piedra for Cesar or Henry. He allowed them to be endangered every minute and every second, not allowing an act of courage to enter his body. After the costly decisions this morning, he let more of his loved ones down.

Right now, he regretfully had to keep apologizing to the two horses he had tied together with the rope slung over his shoulder. He was forced to use the last two bullets in his rifle, one for Taipa and one for Kai. It was the main piece of evidence any of those men back at the crash site had: men escaping on horseback. It wasn't the horses' fault they were run into the canyons in the middle of the night. Jake blamed himself for the loss of their lives, too.

After walking and struggling through the water for twenty minutes, the river became deeper and wider. It became progressively easier for Jake to move the horses. With his exceptional strength, no thanks to El Loto, he was able to make this job move along faster than it normally would have taken any other man.

The current around him was shifting the floor beneath his feet and the first horse behind him nudged him in the back. He had reached the point where he could let them go.

A single green Dodge Staff pulled up next to the pueblo. Winston had been facing it the entire time it was in sight, reminding himself to not look at the valley as long as these officers were here. From the driver side, out stepped a tall and muscular man in a green uniform. He had buzzed grey hair and appeared to be in his fifties. He smiled and waved to Winston. Another man stepped out from the passenger side. This man was twenty years younger than his peer and was dressed in the same apparel. His hair was just as short, but darker, like his presence. Sunglasses hid his eyes from Winston's gaze. The men approached him on the side of the pueblo.

"Howdy, young man," the older one said. Winston noticed how nice their uniforms were as they moved closer. The shoes were shined, round-toed, and black. Each man had a series of medals and honors pressed onto his coat over his left chest. "Do you have a moment to answer some questions?"

Winston stared back at them without saying a word.

The older man cleared his throat. "Do you speak English?"

Winston nodded. "What are you doing here?"

From behind his back, the younger man produced a sheet of paper that he unfolded in front of himself. "Winston Nakai. Ex-Army, part of the Navajo tribe. Is this correct?" His voice was deeper than that of the older official's.

"Yes," Winston replied. He had hoped they wouldn't have been able to pull that information this quickly. These men, as he feared, were part of something larger and more complicated than just the Army. "May I ask again as to why you are here on Reserved land?"

The older man spoke again. "This all yours, Mr. Nakai?" He gestured towards the valley.

He nodded, still not looking towards the valley. "I suppose it is time to give up more of my people's land to you?"

The older one chuckled. "My name is General Thomas Greer. I'm a supervisor at the nearby Army base. This is my partner today, Lieutenant Davis. We come to your territory only wanting answers, not plots of dried land."

Winston spat on the ground in the direction of the two officials. He didn't know of any nearby Army bases. Standing himself up with the assistance of his cane, he said, "You have smokes?"

The younger one, Davis, reached into his back pocket and produced a small red pack, offering a pair of cigarettes. Winston reached and took them, tucking one behind his ear and lighting up the other.

"I'm guessing your being here has something to do with that rattle of gunfire my family woke to last night." Winston was calming down as the cigarette smoke burned its way down to his lungs.

General Greer nodded. "Did you happen to see anything?"

Winston shook his head. "Only heard the big guns go off. My family didn't leave the home."

"I see." Greer examined the pueblo. "How many of you are couped up in there?"

"Five of us. A sixth on the way."

"Wow. Congratulations." It sounded like an empty compliment as he continued to look around the hill. "That's quite a lot of bodies for a small little clay hut like this."

"Life is difficult, General."

"Quite." He walked slowly toward the edge of the hill, investigating the valley now. He took note of the animals he could see from where he stood. "Sheep and chickens staying fed?"

"Hardly," Winston said, as he moved behind Greer.

"Must be difficult for you to manage all this alone. I'm guessing you're receiving benefits still for that wooden foot of yours?"

Winston said nothing. He stared at the ground, trying to avert his eyes and remain calm.

"What's that empty pen down there for?" Davis asked as he stood next to Winston.

"It was a horse corral." Winston dragged his tobacco.

"Was?" asked Greer. "You run this ranch and herd those sheep without any horses? There must be several dozen acres out here. I'm betting that you don't herd with your auto, either? You'd have to drive a bit out of the way to find land flat enough to move that junker down there."

"In this drought, and without any money, the animals start dying, General. I've lost a chicken a week this whole season, now. The horse just passed a few days ago. Lucky that we've only lost one sheep."

"Is that it over there?" Greer pointed towards the canyons where an animal was pitifully rolling around in the dirt. Confused, Winston was forced to look, then saw a dozen military men and pair of Dodge Staffs coming from the north side of his ranch by the canyon. He swallowed the bile rising in his throat, and his shakes began again. They were getting close enough to where he could count how many of them there were. They seemed to come out of nowhere.

"Friends of yours?" Winston asked, trying to keep his voice under control, tasting metal.

"It's routine when you lose the pilot of a shot-down foreign aircraft. As someone that's been in the Army, I think you understand that we don't like to lose things."

"Shot-down aircraft? You're saying there's an enemy pilot that survived, and he's running around the Reservation as we speak? And you haven't found him?"

"Possibly." Greer was turned fully to Winston and grinning. He was waiting for him to break. The Dodges were moving faster, ahead of the men on foot. Within a minute, they'd be by the corrals. "And it is very important that we find this renegade before it gets more out of hand. Your ranch is the closest to the crash site, so we're starting here. Then we'll work our way down the rest of the Reservation until we find what we've been looking for. You're stating that you haven't seen anything, correct?"

"Nothing." Winston shook his head. He saw one of the Army men disappear into the ravine just a couple hundred yards from where Ella and Jake entered. Winston was sweating out of control.

"If you saw something," started Greer, "it'd be advised you spoke up now, son."

Winston watched the men advancing. He tried to come up with something under all the pressure. He didn't want them to find Ella, and he couldn't allow Jake to be found. Hopefully, the horses had floated off and Jake was secure in hiding. He wasn't sure about Ella. Winston couldn't believe that this operation was being so careful. A small militia scanning the ranch. And his property was most likely not the only one receiving this treatment. Something bigger was going on than he knew. And other Natives were now paying the price of his curiosity.

"I saw it," is all Winston muttered.

"Excuse me?" Greer's attitude changed. He appeared thrown off by the admittance.

"I saw it. The plane. I rode out last night to see the crash. My horse broke its leg this morning fleeing the scene, and I was forced to bury it behind the stable."

Davis and Greer exchanged glances. They seemed surprised by all this. Winston was still staring at the approaching Army men.

"Can we please go somewhere else to talk?" Winston asked. "I don't want my children to see any of this. We're simple folk, General."

Greer took a deep breath in. "Okay. Come with us. We'll straighten it all out and bring you back to your family afterwards." He signaled to Davis. "Communicate down to J.R. that we found something."

Davis nodded. He pulled a walkie off his belt loop and murmured instructions into it. Greer stood behind Winston and urged him towards the car, and the three of them drove down towards the town of Magdalena.

Her head was aching horribly. She had lost her footing in panic and had fallen backwards down into the stream. The back of her skull had smacked a large rock right where the water began. She sat up and touched the back of her head to feel the tenderness buried underneath her long, wet hair. No blood, thankfully, but she could already feel it swelling.

Clambering her way steadily back up the rocky incline to the valley, she could see stars in her vision. She had hit her head harder than she realized. She squeezed her eyes tight, trying to regain her focus. She knew men were marching this way, just as Jake promised they would. Easing her way to where the land flattened out, she peered over to see two green cars parked by the sheep corral. Several men in dark green uniforms, their sleeves rolled up to their elbows, were walking around the ranch, surveying the layout. Off to her right in the distance, a couple of the uniformed men were standing over what looked like a dead animal. A sheep. At least, she thought it was dead until one of them suddenly pulled a handgun out and shot down at the motionless creature.

She held her breath. Her head was pounding as she tried to remain still and not be noticed. She was still several acres from the nearest man. It would be difficult for anyone to make out the top of her head from that distance. She craned her neck to look back up to the hill where the pueblo was, but still didn't see anybody up there. *"I wonder if they took Winston?"* she asked herself. She watched the group of men search the property, praying nobody would come as far as the riverbed…

She heard a splash in the water. Multiple. Coming from the north where the men entered the valley. She froze. There were only a few bushes and a couple low trees for her cover along the creek. She was mostly exposed where she was. She stretched her neck out towards the stream to see a single uniformed man just hundred or so feet away. He was shin-deep in the water as his sturdy shoes stomped down, splashing about a whole lot of noise. He wasn't trying to be sneaky.

Ella frantically looked around her, not knowing where to go. Right now, just enough dried brush was obstructing his view of her. If she were to move away from him, the movement alone would sound the alarm.

"Jake, where are you?" The man was close now. Just several seconds away from standing directly in front of her. She remained

a stone. She could see that he was scanning the water for something. Possibly anything that could help them find what they were looking for. But why was he walking in the water?

She could feel her heart racing. At first, she thought about making a run for it. But she couldn't decide where. This was the worst-case scenario she and Jake discussed before he took the two horses down the river. He had told her to just hope nobody came down the embankment while he was gone. She wished to have joined Jake in getting away from Winston's land, but the embankment disappears around the bend, leaving her to fight the growing strength of current where Jake had to reach with the horses. She would have caused more of a fuss if she had gone with him. But of course, someone was searching the river. She had no self-defense. She couldn't fight a soldier that was likely well-trained. Why did this have to happen? Everything started to go dark. Her vision was tunneling. She was about to faint. And she played it to her advantage.

The man hurried his way next to her body once he saw her. She was unconscious. His face was contorted with confusion, and he checked to see what could be wrong with this randomly placed white woman next to a river on the Reservation. He checked her pulse. She was alive, her hair was wet, but her clothes weren't.

The official was a thirty-some aged man with scruff on his face. He wore a hat that protected his bald head from the sun. He took it off momentarily to wipe away sweat. He had kind eyes and was standing himself up to yell to his team for assistance. As he was about to reach his full height, something behind him splashed aggressively across the stream. He turned around and saw something hideous charging at him: a mutant of some sort. Before he could process what it was or make a sound to call for help, the monster lunged at him, knocking him on his back and covering his mouth to prevent any sound from escaping.

The monster, which looked like a human with scales for skin, had pinned him to the side of the slope. The weight of the being for its height did not make sense. The man on the ground had no leverage against the creature atop him.

Jake didn't know what to do. He effortlessly held down the officer, trying to search his mind for an answer to the predicament. Ella was just coming to, behind him. He shushed her as she sat up and groaned. She saw that Jake had the man from the water subdued.

Climbing her way up beside Jake, she asked, "What are you going to do to him?"

"I don't know," Jake said. "What happened to you?"

"I had a fainting spell."

"Are you okay?"

Ella nodded. She could see the fear in the man's eyes as he stared up at Jake. How terrifying it must be to see something unhuman like that. He kept jerking his body, thinking he could catch Jake off guard and best him. He didn't have a chance.

"He keeps trying to scream out," Jake said. "I can't trust him." Jake stared directly down at the officer. Jake's eyes were a golden-red color, sort of amber-like. A beautiful color, but not in the eyes of the beast that has overpowered you. To the man on his back, it was like looking up at the real Medusa. He was trembling, knowing certainly what this monster was about to do.

"Go find a rock," Jake said regretfully to Ella. "A heavy one..."

Ella hesitated but did as she was asked. A minute later, Jake was apologizing yet again to another living being for being put in the middle of a situation he had started. Another living being that was to be no more.

08

July 1947
Magdalena, New Mexico

THE WAITRESS FINISHED POURING THE CUPS OF COFFEE FOR THE TWO SOLDIERS AND THE MYSTERIOUS INDIAN FACING THEM. The diner in the town of Magdalena was empty except for a couple old men that sat at the countertop on red and white stools. A radio played jazz tunes over the intercom for the guests, drowning out the loud sizzle of the grill coming from the large window that opened into the kitchen.

It was just an hour to noon, and Winston had already sweated through his long sleeve button-up. Thankfully, the dark red color of the material disguised most of the stains. He used the last of Davis's smokes on the ride down from the top of the hill, and he had acquired a hard cough that was sure to last most of the rest of the day. He had not been looking at the men since they sat down. He was nervous and scared. He had convinced them to come to this diner. A public setting, just so he wouldn't be alone with them. They agreed, and were charmed at the idea, as if they were longtime friends of his, wanting to catch up.

Winston kept thinking to himself how odd this interrogation session was: in the middle of a town, witnesses all around, and sitting across from two military officers that just invaded his ranch in search of answers to a problem he created. They had supposedly called off their search right as they were leaving

Winston's land. But he did not believe that to be true. He'd hoped for Jake and Ella to be somewhere far away and for none of the officials back at the ranch to be looking for the phony horse grave behind the stable he had told Greer and Davis about.

When he asked the two officers to come here to talk, he thought it would be an easier atmosphere to receive his questioning. But because these two were acting smug, he couldn't understand their angle.

Greer tipped the coffee mug to his lips, licking them after in satisfaction with the dark bitter taste. "The papers say rain could be weeks away, still. Lots of ranchers from here to Flagstaff are going to struggle mightily for some time. Thank God for the heavy frost melt and rains up in Colorado. At least some water is making it down this way." He sipped his coffee again. "I took notice of your field and livestock. I'm guessing you haven't been receiving compensation for your services. Or you're spending it unwisely. But something tells me you're smarter than that."

Winston kept staring down into his coffee cup. He was chewing on his bottom lip and gave a subtle nod.

"We can help you, son," Greer went on. "We can relieve you of all your worries. Your animals can be fed again. Your family. We can find out why your benefits stopped and resume them from here on until they are exhausted. And all those checks you never received, we can combine into one large payment that will save everything you've worked hard for. In return, I think you know what we're asking from you, first."

Greer stared generously at Winston. He looked up to meet Greer's eyes. All that was said and promised meant little to Winston right now. Yes, it would grant him the quality of a slightly better life. It would be easier to continue working on his ranch and maintain cash flow. He was too embarrassed to admit it to his family or Jake, but it had been some time since he last received pay from the government. However, he remained worried about anything they could find back at his ranch. He believed the men continued searching his property, contrary to what these two said to him.

"Why did you lie to us at first, Mr. Nakai?" Davis asked. "You said you didn't leave your home when you heard the gunfire. But now, when we called in our team to investigate your property, you seemed eager to get us away from there. Tell us what you saw. This is your own military you are potentially conspiring against." He poured some sugar into his coffee and stirred aggressively. He appeared to be holding back much more emotion than Greer was. At least, his impatience was more evident.

Winston took a deep breath, buying time to gather his story. "I was the only Indian in my barracks, Lieutenant. I was bullied everyday throughout my training at base camp. Kicked around, teased, mocked. I wasn't as tough-skinned as the others. I'd lose control some nights and cry to myself, which emboldened them to come after me more.

"I didn't know what the war was going to be like. I never held a gun before. I had no want to kill. I joined the Army because it was still a better life than I had on the Reservation. My parents died when I was fifteen, from alcohol abuse. My older sister helped me survive. She was good at beading and crafting. We would go find where the people were around New Mexico and Colorado and sell what we could just to get some food in our stomachs. We traveled on horseback everywhere."

"You rode horses all over New Mexico and Colorado?" Davis asked. He was genuinely surprised.

"Yes. We couldn't afford a car. And we weren't going to trade in my father's or mother's horses to help us. It would be unfair to the animals. They are not a currency, in my family's beliefs. And I also named my father's horse when I was thirteen. It was sentimental to me."

"I'm sorry Mr. Nakai, this is wasting a great deal of time—"

Greer put his hand up to Davis, pausing his thought. "Go on, son. I take it the horse you just lost earlier this morning was one that belonged to your parents?"

Winston nodded. He was telling the truth. "Taipa, was his name. My father's horse. Then there was my sister, who was my best friend, killed by the bite of a rattlesnake two years after my parents were buried. I was alone in the world. I didn't know much about anything. I didn't have my sister's ability to craft. And I couldn't trap anything for trade. That's what my parents did. Trapped and traded pelts and skins. I was lucky enough to come upon Enola, now my wife. It is her parents' pueblo we now live in. She too had recently lost her family, and she was in desperate need of help as well. We saved each other.

"I'm no good at ranching, General. That's why I joined the Army. I'm no good at anything, it seems. What I've been meaning to say this whole time is, when I finally went out to do something for the good of others around me, my peers in the Army treated me like dirt. They disliked me very much when I did nothing wrong." He paused. "Do you know how I lost my foot?"

"I do not, Private," said Greer. His face showed genuine concern. Davis started flipping through the folder papers again that must have contained Winston's record.

Winston sipped his coffee for the first time. It was lukewarm. "When my squad dropped in France, they thought it was a fun game to make me dance. Once, sometimes twice a day, their pistols would be aimed at my feet and fired inches from them. Worst of all, our commanding officer was in on the fun. Nobody backed me. Nobody was on my side. The fun and games ended for them after a few weeks of marching when one of their bullets traveled from behind my toes and out the arch of my foot. I fell. Some of them argued with each other as I was rolling in pain. Others fought laughs.

"What happened next was the culminations of their actions meeting consequence. An explosion went off at the front of the group, sending some of them flying. Our commanding officer had stumbled upon a mine. Clumsy bastard. Was too busy enjoying my anguish to watch for the lumps in the ground. I was dragged out by my peers into a nearby ditch. I wasn't the only one to survive and lose a part of me. It was also one of the last days I was in Europe before being evacuated. I never told the truth of what happened that day. But that's because no one ever asked. They wouldn't have cared.

"That's why I felt no need to tell you anything back at my home, General. The Army was nothing but nasty to me. Treated me like a second-class citizen, just as my people have been for over a century. My relationship with people like you was severed a *long* time ago. Don't blame me for telling a lie to the people who crippled me."

There was silence for a moment as the officers took in what Winston was saying. Davis closed the folder and nodded to Greer, as if informing him that Winston's story checks out.

Winston spoke again. This time, with more gumption. "I don't believe you'll give me anything if I tell you anything. I'm not sure what else there is to tell, except that you were on my land, looking to find my beloved horse that I had to put down because of my curiosity over the commotion near my land. Now, we're here, and you're wanting to pick my brain to see how much I saw."

They remained silent, sipping their coffees.

"I did go down to the crash site. Twice. The first time to

check on Mr. Foreman. And a second time to get my rifle to kill that Jap in the plane. Then I waited for you to come this morning. I searched everywhere for a bone in my body that would allow me to trust in telling you anything. Trying to think of what I could do that could keep my family safe and away from your nonsense. Well, there you have it. You scared it all out of me, because I don't want you people anywhere near me or my family."

Greer whistled softly and bowed his head. Davis scratched the back of his head and signaled the waitress over to their table to get the check.

"We apologize, Mr. Nakai," said General Greer. "We'll look to better handle situations like this in the future." He looked at Davis, who used his thumb to wipe an imaginary line from the lobe of his ear down to his chin. A signal. "We will get you your money. All of it. Everything that you missed. We appreciate your coming here with us. It was a pleasure."

Like a shotgun blast, the front door to the diner swung open and banged hard against the wall. A man came lurching into the diner, his face was red, and he looked furious.

It was Joe Foreman.

"*'Ere you are!*" He yelled in the direction of Winston and the two officers. His voice sounded funny. Something was inside his mouth making it difficult for him to speak. "*'Ose are deh meh who have deh 'pace arien! 'Dem right 'ere!*"

Then Winston remembered; his tongue was gone! He had bitten it off earlier this morning, and by the looks of it, gauze was balled up in his mouth. The two old guys in the diner turned around to look at Greer and Davis, along with the waitress and the cook from beyond the window. The two officials were alert now as everyone's eyes were on them.

"*'Dey dook me home las' nigh'! 'Dey had one of 'dem ariens! Id adacked! An undodly creadur!*"

Davis hurried forward into action. "Nothing to see here, folks. He's delusional." He reached out to Foreman, trying to push him out the door. They wrestled for a minute, and they had a heated exchange loudly between them, talking over each other. It was difficult to make anything out exactly.

Greer turned to Winston. "Here's some money for the coffee. I think we're done here. But you do know for a fact that it *was* a Japanese pilot you killed?"

Winston looked between the action happening by the door. Davis was pushing Foreman outside as he continued to yell. Winston looked back to Greer. "Yes. Who else could it have been?"

Greer flashed a smile. "Don't worry about any of it. Thank you for putting a bullet in our enemy. We're handling the situation so, just keep quiet, and your money will make it to you. Nobody will bother you again." He extended his hand to shake Winston's. "Here's some change. You'll need to find your own way back home, unfortunately."

With that, Greer rushed out towards Davis, who was forcing Old Man Foreman into the back of the Green Dodge Staff Winston had arrived in.

"That's the third one this week." The waitress appeared behind him at his table. She was an older lady with bright red lipstick that was so liberally applied, it was spotted on her teeth.

Winston was even more confused than he had been previously. Did he just get away with all those lies? "I'm sorry, what did you say?"

"Aliens. Creatures from the sky. Supposedly, they've been taking people then returning them after a while. Jessie Denard and Wilt Mullins both claimed it happened to them. They were arrested earlier this week for having outbursts just like that." She stared down at him. "Those two friends of yours?"

Winston shrugged. "Colleagues."

"Hm. Well, I'm glad someone is handling the loonies in this town. Need any change" She grabbed the bill off the table. Winston shook his head, watching the Dodge drive out of sight.

"*So many lies*," he thought. He never danced for any man.

09

July 1947
Alamo Indian Reservation

WINSTON JUMPED OUT FROM THE BACK OF A RED PICKUP TRUCK. He circled around to the driver side and handed an old Indian man the fifty cents that Greer had left for him back at the diner. He had been gracious enough to provide Winston a ride back to his home.

"*Ahéhee'*," Winston thanked the old man. The man smiled and gestured a goodbye wave as he prepared himself to drive back towards town.

Winston's family was waiting for him outside the pueblo. The children rushed over to him and entangled him in their arms, gleeful as their father returned home safely. Enola walked over with a smile on her face and joined in the embrace.

"Please, Winston," she said. "Don't give them a reason to return."

"I'm sorry," said Winston. "I make a promise to you that no unwelcomed man will step foot onto our land again."

He relaxed for the first time since he had been awakened by Jake early this morning, lying beside his wife and his beloved children on the cozy pile of blankets and wool padding they used as one large bed. That moment was short-lived when he realized that two other members of his family were not in his presence.

"Where's Jake and Ella?" He looked at the area around him.

"They must still be down by the creek," Enola responded.

Winston released his family, then hobbled over to the side of the hill overlooking his valley. There was no sign of them anywhere.

"When did they leave? The Army men?"

Enola came up behind him, shading her eyes to help her see out towards the edge of the valley. "They turned around just a few minutes after you had gone."

Winston sighed heavily, which led to a short coughing fit. He picked his way down the hillside, and readied himself to make a long, tiring journey to the creek. On one and half feet, it would take him nearly half an hour to reach the stream.

He tried to ignore the feelings that were threatening to overcome him regarding his horse. His job was going to be harder without Taipa, now. And his mother's horse that Jake rode, Kai, was gone too. Taipa, meaning "spread wings", once belonged to his father. He died not in vain. He did not deserve death, but the sacrifice saved the people in Winston's life. Taipa did not know why he had to die, which made it harder for Winston to convince himself on this long walk that Taipa had to be killed.

"*Circumstance.*" Winston dropped a single tear from his eye. "*If only I could justify his death, rightfully.*"

———————

He reached the creek, only to find another problem placed at his feet. Jake and Ella were sitting on the rocks by the water. A man in green uniform was sprawled out in front of them.

"What the hell happened?" Winston demanded,

Jake remained seated and kept looking down at the dead body of the officer. "Are the rest of them gone?"

"Not for long! Once they do roll call, they'll be marching back down to this valley wondering where they lost a man. How could you be so stupid?"

Jake glared at Winston. "If you come down here, you'll see that I've got it figured out."

Winston controlled his frustration and walked down to the dead man. He could see he had blood trickling from his skull, with a slightly bruised indentation on his temple.

"We had to, Winston," said Ella. "He came down here and saw me. Jake had to do what he did."

"Look at this luck we finally ran into, though," Jake said.

"Luck?" Winston was on the verge of a raging fit. As he got closer, he saw a rattlesnake pinned under Jake's foot. It was still alive and rattling.

"It came out of that hole over there, right after it happened. I picked it up and saw an opportunity to wipe our hands clean."

"Did it bite him?"

"Right in the shin. After some guidance from myself."

"So, what? His men are going to come back here. I promised my family that those people would never come back. Don't you see how much suspicion this is going to raise?"

"I'll explain everything to Enola," said Ella. "She'll understand. She'll have to."

"I figure that they'll come looking," said Jake, "then they find the body, see the bites, see there's a hole for a snake not ten feet away, and they won't investigate any further. Just another idiot that got too close to the coil of a deadly animal."

Winston sighed. "Whatever happens, we must be on high alert. You two need to stay low and be ready." He swore. "How do you explain the bloody temple?"

Jake placed his boot on the side of the man's head and turned it, so that the bloody part was running into the river. Next to his head, some large rocks. "He lost his footing after being shocked by the bite. He hit his head, doing most of the damage. Then the venom's effects attacked him while unconscious." Jake stood up and stood next to Winston. The rattlesnake slithered its way loose and was moving slowly towards its hole, keeping an eye on Jake and Winston. "We can't hide anything this time. We need them to come here to see it for themselves. They can draw the obvious conclusion."

Winston turned around and crawled his way up the steep embankment. "If you want to remain in hiding, stop lighting fires for everyone to see. Start acting like a survivor, Snake Boy."

Jake hung his head low. Guilt overwhelmed him once more.

At the top of the hill, Winston turned around. "If this does blow over, you're going to go find us some new horses."

Jake nodded his head, grateful for a friend as kind as Winston Nakai. He would do anything to regain the bond he surely challenged over the past eight hours.

Conclusion

July 1947
New Mexico

THE ARMY MEN RETURNED LATER THAT DAY. Howbeit, they never came to Winston's front step. From the corral, Winston had watched a small search team stroll beside the riverbed, until they found who they were looking for. In a matter of minutes, Jake's plan and hypothesis must have worked. The group of soldiers, officers, whatever they were, turned around immediately after discovering the body.

Better yet, many days had passed, and the Nakai pueblo decided it was safe for Jake and Ella to resurface from the home. They resumed work on the ranch; sheering sheep, selling eggs and poultry (conservatively), as they always had. The money that Greer and Davis had promised came within a month, saving many of the starving animals just in time. The rains came just after that, replenishing the fields with grass for the animals, as well.

Jake had begun construction of a small wooden house on the hill next to Winston's pueblo. After getting the bare bones of the structure built, he had surprised Winston with a pair of gifts: two new ponies. They were both still fillies, but they were energetic and had strong builds. A young Palomino, and a Morgan that resembled Taipa.

As everything in Winston's life seemed to be dawning a brighter horizon, he replayed the conversation with Greer and Davis in the Magdalena diner every day in his head, for months after it happened. "*Aliens*," they had said. Two people spoke that word in under a minute's time, separate from each other's conversations. He wasn't sure what they meant by it. The waitress very well was going off hearsay. But Foreman, the old white farmer that was attacked by that thing in the wreck, had disappeared after he said that word. His land had been sold off a couple months after the incident. His wife hadn't been heard from by anyone in the town since that day, either. When Enola would go into town around the time the Foreman land went up for sale, she tried to find out what happened to the couple.

Nobody knew anything.

The word, "alien", meant something. It bothered Winston and Jake. They tried to avoid the topic as best they could. But with the search party that came, and the uniqueness of the being in the plane, the disappearances of an old local couple, and the arrests of so called "loonies" in the town, it was discouraging knowing that something else was going on out there. More so now that every month after the incident, the term "space alien" was appearing in the papers in a story. "SIGHTINGS OF SPACEMEN" or, "FALLEN ANGELS", "DEMONS FROM ABOVE", "FLYING SAUCER CRAZE" and "FOO FIGHTER". Headlines that sold an impressive amount of newsprint. People would surface to their local authorities with outlandish stories of themselves or relatives being kidnapped from the sky. Or they would see ominous apparitions that were non-human moving around their properties. More and more, the papers began to feel like tabloids. Reader bait, as Ella called it. Meant to rile the people up.

Not long after these stories began to make headlines, there was a decline of interest people had in the papers. Deeper into the irrelevant pages of "news" the stories went. And soon, it was as if they never happened. The term "alien" stuck, and many people played into the fairytale, developing it as a sort of cultural phenomenon.

The canyons also reminded Winston of those events that one day. It reminded him of the weird and fearful time that started all this chatter. A plane crash, one with multiple witnesses, tiptoed its way around the newspapers. The *real* occurrence that never was publicly reported. A possible foreign air attack that happened in a rural area that was nothing more than a rumor for a very short time. The foreigner inside had looked human enough, but something about it never sat right with Jake or Winston.

He lost his parent's horses that day. His land was invaded. His family was put in harm's way. It was the most frightening day since Winston lost his foot from a landmine set off by his Captain.

"*How grey this world is becoming*," Winston thought.

Conspiracy
In Action

Part 1

<u>Camelot</u>

Summer 1954
Geneva, Switzerland

HEAVY CEDAR DOORS A MILE HIGH SWUNG OPEN, RELEASING THE TENSION BUILT UP BEHIND THEM. A conference room full of suits with ties shifted uncomfortably to the words echoing off the walls. Words that were peaceful in their delivery, but fierce in nature. The square room held the representatives of several different nations, all listening to the single voice, impatiently awaiting an end to a speech that resulted in one man's unexpected departure from the conference.

The titanic doors closed behind him. Though they weren't large doors to begin with, they appeared God-sized to a man such as himself. Practically running away from a room possessed by people that had the ability to wipe away the Earth with just a few simple words, he never turned back towards those gates as the hallway was silenced at their shutting. No longer could he hear the kings and demi-gods behind him dispute each ideological version of how this planet shall be ruled.

Bald, stout, sweaty, and uncharacteristically nervous; these are the most relevant words at the time to describe the fleeing gentleman. Muttering under his breath as his short legs propelled him down the hallway, he had to collect the facts before recounting his story over the phone call that surely awaited him back in his hotel room.

He pushed his way out the front doors into the Suisse summer air. Heavy and thick, the heat dragged him down more as he was met by his peers at the entrance to the Palace of Nations. Two men dressed in black suits, black ties, black fedoras, and somehow featuring blacker eyes walked behind him down the steps to their idling vehicle, each of their footsteps coordinated to mirror the other's. Left foot, right foot, left foot, right foot—creating the illusion that only one man was following.

"Blast!" The bald man blurted. "Blasted, bloody bastards! Hurry me away from here! Back to the Inn! Now!"

The men in black did not respond. They followed their boss down to the line of cars on the front driveway, all idling quietly, awaiting their leaders. His driver smoothly opened the door to his black Rolls Royce.

"Is Sir Milton accompanying?" The chauffer asked.

"No! Bloody leave him," responded the bald man. "He'll find his own way around."

"As you wish, Doctor."

The man plumped into the back seat with one of his associates, the other sitting up front with the driver. As soon as the car began pulling away from the Palace, the bald Brit, Dr. Alexander Erickson, started swearing and shaking his head at every thought that swirled through his mind. The suited man in the passenger seat turned around, removing his hat and revealing straight dark hair. He only stared as he waited for the bald man's explanation for this abrupt departure.

"It's happening," said Dr. Erickson. "China is going rogue. The accords were sloppy. Nobody can expect peace from this."

"What do you mean 'China is going rogue'?" the deep, American voice of the man in the front seat growled.

"It wants to see a change in the world. The President, his cabinet of slimy dragons, all of those East Asian separatists.

Bastards!" His heavy breathing became the only noise in the cab over the accelerating engine. The men in black stared at him with their soulless eyes, letting him catch his breath before he elaborated on what he had heard in the closed-door meeting. "Not a good change for us. He wants *his* vision of sovereign Asia to be recognized. Away from the rest of the globe, isolated under his legacy's rule, against everything we've been trying to achieve the past forty years."

"We knew he was becoming a problem," said the low voice. "Are you saying it's too late for us to save?"

"Blah. He's taking other names with him is what's difficult. Khrushchev, Sihanouk, Sasorith. Even bloody Churchill!"

"Churchill doesn't share the same ideas as any of those names."

"It's different for him, I do believe. It's a matter of independence. And to break up what we've been constructing through the years. He's a known enemy to many of our friends and associates, and I think his stance is controversial on purpose, to get France and the lot of 'em out of Vietnam."

"We can't afford to lose that territory now."

"We might as well prepare for a losing conflict then." Erickson wiped his forehead clear of the sweat building up. The beautiful mountainous scenery of the Suisse Alps was sparking solutions to their new problems, providing inspiration as the vehicle crawled forward. "The French are too weak and unpredictable to keep in South Vietnam. We need a powerful body that we can trust and rely on to win back our order without starting a third World War."

The associate to his left spoke for the first time. A thin Germanic accent seething from his teeth. "This is going to set us back a half-century if Mai-Xeng splits from the *Diadems* and takes the Soviets with him. We'll lose several legs of the *Atlas*, and with it, the ability to advance the globe to our New World. Everything will crumble if this continues. What is it that we can do to immediately change the guard of South Vietnam before China and President Mai-Xeng secure more allies?"

Dr. Erickson was red with rage. He had tried not to mention the downfall of his people's government. He was high up within his Brothers' council, nearly to the top of power. Not only was he in charge of making world-saving or world-ending decisions, but his life was also in the hands of the masters at the very top; the Diadems. He had attended this conference in Switzerland to observe and report, to strategize and manipulate, only to hear that suddenly it all could be over for him.

"Are you sure there isn't a way to swing Churchill to our favor? His backing could be paramount." asked the man in the front seat.

Erickson shook his head. "Not without his diving further into our business. Especially now if we are being divided, he could rally enough allies to fully eliminate us."

The doctor's eyes were bulging in his fury, his emotions boiling. The two men never turned their eyes from him as the car glided its way back to their hotel in Champel in the center of Geneva; their lives were safe. They obeyed, and they had unwavering loyalty to The Diadems. Following every order, these shady figures were highly skilled, extremely dangerous, and the closest a human can get to immortality. Erickson's life was, at present, in their hands.

He spoke again: "If Mai-Xeng were any more foolish, we'd have a chance at replacing him. To think, after all the safeguards the Brothers have put in place through the years—"

"Careful, Dr. Erickson," said the German to his left. "There is no need to place blame anywhere beyond yourself, at this point. So far as I've sat adjacent to you, I'd deem you nothing less than a failure in today's agenda."

"The only one to blame is that snake Mai-Xeng," Erickson said, quickly defending himself.

The two men nodded once in an intimidating approval. Erickson was the fool who misspoke in this moment. The rage filled his face with heat so hot, tears were building in his eyes. At least, he tried to convince himself that it was rage causing the pooling tears. He could almost see the strings above the men in black being held in place by his Older Brothers, waiting for them to act in one swift movement to remove him from the living. A bullet to the brain? A slit of the throat?

He had no family or friends. At fifty-years old and having a devilish thirst for power, he operated as a machine, devoting his life to the wealth and agenda of the world sought best by the Diadems. Erickson was in a perfect place of deep-rooted power for them to use, and he welcomed every luxury that came with following their path. As a Health Specialist working for the United Kingdom at the World Health Organization, he worked alongside many powerful friends, and few enemies. Though he loved Mother England, where he had lived most of his childhood before moving to Denmark, he spent years studying for his Doctorate in epidemiology. His lifelong goal was to be one of the heroes that could prevent or end the next Bubonic Plague. His mind was great, and his attention to detail was just as. His hundreds of published essays and theorems are what got him recognized by the WHO. All his works were related to recognizing patterns of symptoms, statistics, and the location of outbreaks for nearly every known disease in the world. He was so meticulous in his ways, the WHO and every employer before, quickly had him on their radars.

Eventually, he landed himself on others' radars as well. He became entwined with people that wanted to know him, specifically within Parliament. Through them, his connections grew, and the wealthier the man he befriended, the better the bond was between them. The more he was slowly groomed into this shadow industry of elites, the higher the status he experienced, becoming just one of many trying to manipulate a globe best fit for the future of man and Brothers.

The Rolls Royce parked across the street from their hotel, when the tension inside Erickson was at its peak. He knew he was at a point where he was considerably too important to be killed by his peers. But with something as altering as a major shift in the global power structure, his decisions had to be sharp and punctual. He said this:

"I'll get our people in front of Eisenhower. We can still save these castle walls from falling. Build them back up stronger, in the meantime. And I know just the architect."

He exhaled quietly, the pressure slowly releasing from his temples. After a minute of sitting in silence, the dark-dressed men averted their attention from him for the first time. He exhaled quietly once more, stepped carefully out of the car and readied himself to make the most important telephone call of his life.

Part 2

<u>Affair</u>

Summer 1954

Camp David, Maryland

WITHOUT ANY BREEZE THIS EARLY EVENING, THE GOLF BALL SOARED STRAIGHT TOWARDS THE PIN, LANDING AND KICKING UP A DIVOT TEN FEET FROM THE HOLE.

Standing tall and proud, the golfer puffed on his cigarette and grinned. He is an old man looking sharp in the appropriate golf apparel; white collared shirt, khaki slacks, and rounded brown spikes comforting his feet. The day was perfect: no wind, warm air, no cloud in sight, only a few birds could be heard chirping in the trees. Silence. Silent was how he liked it when he came outside to his custom backyard course. All problems seemed to fade to the back of his mind when he had the time to come out here and hit his round with a small sycophantic crowd of Service Men quietly approving of his play, way behind him on the deck of his house.

He had just returned from Switzerland and needed an escape for a weekend. Tensions in Asia were rising, and he knew something major was looming on the horizon. His job was about to become busier and more difficult the moment he left the serenity of this resort. Between the convention's somewhat failure at finding a resolution to French-colonial presence in Vietnam, and the new aggressions being taken by the Chinese President, the world was going to turn its attention to the United States. As its President, Dwight Eisenhower needed these couple of days to find solace before he was to deal with it all. And there was no better peace within his mind than he felt staring across the green rolling fields of short-bladed grass, admiring the beauty of nature's living carpet receiving the little white ball that exploded from the tee box.

"Wonderful shot, Mr. President," said a man from behind him. He was a little younger and dressed for the game in green plaid head to toe. If he were to walk into the tree line, he'd surely blend in without effort in that attire. Though he wasn't to join his Commander and Chief to play this round, he volunteered to carry his President's clubs rather, in hopes that his playing alone would silence his demons. "Should be a birdie, without question."

"On a day like today, Kurt, I cannot, and will not, miss," said Eisenhower. They were walking down to the green and Eisenhower stomped out his cigarette in the grass, striking up a new one.

"Keeping that habit out of Mamie's line of sight, I'd hope," said Kurt, sarcastically.

"As long as she's still drinking, I'll keep smoking. She probably won't be able to put a bottle down long enough to see me, anyhow."

Kurt Jameson was a good friend of Eisenhower. More so since being asked into the Eisenhower cabinet, elevating him from his previous position inside of Congress. After never having met the President before Eisenhower hit the campaign trail a couple of years back, he had been at the side of the President almost every day since. Whether it be a morning coffee in the Presidential Quarters, field trips across the country, or a weekend swinging clubs here at Camp David, Jameson was, in his mind, very close to and trusted by the President.

Eisenhower lined up his putt, the cigarette cocked out of the corner of his lips, eyeing his recently constructed green for the perfect line. Once his breath was steady and wrists were relaxed, he swung gently back, then forth, striking the ball directly into the hole.

"Another wonderful shot, sir," said Jameson.

"Just as smooth as I can lead this country, Kurt," Eisenhower let out a laugh. But that laugh was soon cut short, as the atmosphere around them vibrated and beat out an unnatural fluttering; the spinning blades from an approaching helicopter entering the area. They both looked back towards the house where the aircraft landing pad awaited the lowering chopper.

"Were you expecting guests?" Jameson asked.

"Not in the slightest." He dragged hard on his cigarette.

Two members of the Secret Service walked over to the tee box of the hole they were playing, dressed as casually as if they were on vacation here, as well: khaki shorts, cotton polos, sunglasses. They waited for Jameson and the President at the hilltop, summoning for them without a word leaving their lips.

"Who do we have coming here disrupting my vacation?' Eisenhower hollered to the Service members once they reached them.

"They called in just thirty minutes ago, sir," said the young Service member. "They said it was urgent and needed an immediate summit with your people."

"Well, my people aren't here. This couldn't have waited until Monday?"

"I think once you see who's here, Mr. President, you'll understand."

"Who—" Eisenhower peered towards the helicopter and who was stepping out. He frowned and was extremely displeased at who appeared. "God dammit. I thought I was done with these snakes for a while."

Together, the Service Men escorted Secretary Jameson and President Eisenhower back to the house at Camp David.

————————————

Sitting around a cozy, cabin-like living space, the President and Kurt Jameson were forced to entertain these two guests. The first man was short and middle-aged, had slicked back hair and dressed in a very expensive two-piece suit. He had a mole pushed directly into the side of one cheek that happened to be the only thing unattractive about his face. Eisenhower spotted a watch as wide as a golf ball on his wrist when this man reached forward to the coffee table for his sweet tea.

This man was Senator Adam Elder of Louisiana. Democrat, segregationist, spending most of his political time "*keeping the blacks at bay*". Eisenhower despised him. Many times these two were at each other's throats when it came to military spending and social issues. And the President couldn't find any other excuse except a hostile one that brought Elder here today.

The only other person who had arrived with Elder was far more unnerving for Jameson and Eisenhower. Dressed in a black suit, shiny black shoes, black fedora (which he rudely kept on indoors), and no jewelry (unless you counted the obsidians he had for eyes). "Shadow Men" is how politicians around the world referred to people like him. The two hosts knew little about who they were and why they were often around the same few politicians. Even some businessmen had these inscrutable characters following them everywhere.

The eeriest part was that they all looked and dressed the same. Carbon copies of each other, almost. Clones working quietly amongst powerful friends or employers. Jameson thought to himself how these Shadow Men acted like the devil on everyone's shoulders. And that they always happened to be accompanying someone that Jameson personally never got along with. He was sure Eisenhower felt the same.

"To what do I owe this pleasure, Senator?" Eisenhower began the conversation with clear discontent in his voice.

Sipping his tea as if purposely attempting to create a dramatic moment, Elder responded eventually with that deep southern accent of his: "Matters well above your paygrade, Dwight."

Tension was instantly injected into the room. Eisenhower felt disrespected on his home turf by a smaller politician. But given the escort of the Shadow Man, he knew Senator Elder was probably right.

"Excuse your tone, Adam," Jameson stepped in.

Eisenhower raised his hand and shook his head, warning his friend of running his mouth any further. "Go on, Senator. Tell me what is on the table. It better be worth the disruption of my game."

Making himself comfortable, with a smirk he said, "I'm sure you are aware that the conference in Geneva did not go as planned."

Eisenhower nodded. "Of course."

"Poorly executed on your part, if I do say so myself," Elder went on.

Jameson bit his tongue. The President's face was turning pink.

"President Mai-Xeng isn't bluffing, you know," Elder said. "He has the global axis at its tipping point. We think he'll see his threats out, whether it results in a third World War or not." He sipped his tea slowly again. "It's difficult to say where his motive lies in isolating Asia from the rest of the world. Some of us believe he couldn't care less about the people of Asia, and that he is just doing it to secure a forever legacy surrounding his family. You know, exactly what has inspired Asian empires to rise historically. But others that are closer to the matter claim Mai-Xeng is trying to challenge us into—"

"Why would he challenge the U.S. directly?" Jameson interrupted. "The French are the ones causing the conflict over there."

"If you were any more enlightened, which you gladly aren't, you'd understand that I wasn't referring to 'us' as the United Sates. That, Mr. Jameson, is very, very high above *your* paygrade."

"Why do you think you can come in here and insult us like this?" Jameson barked at Elder.

"Quiet, Kurt!" Eisenhower snapped.

"Mr. President, they are offending us in your own home—"

"Leave now!" Eisenhower yelled. "I will take care of the business here. You go wait down by the links. I'll see you down there soon. Hopefully."

With his mouth gaping, in awe that he was being thrown out of the "big boy conversation", he stood up, slammed the rest of his coffee, then stormed out. Dejected and confused, he swore many times under his breath on his way out the door.

"I'm sorry for the interruptions," Eisenhower said, now calmed down. "There won't be any more, I can promise that."

Again, sipping his tea with extreme satisfaction, Elder was not hiding this power rush he was feeling. "Your friend isn't too bright. Yet, you keep him close. Good on you."

"Please, tell me why you're here, Adam."

"The Diadems, Dwight. You should know that by now, whenever I must go out of my way to speak to the likes of you, it's never going to be about *you*. But rather men much more important. And they are uneasy at the moment. The separation that is seemingly inevitable in Asia has raised another alarm around the world that we could be entering another major war in the coming years. A war our people were not anticipating. The Brotherhood not only fears for the future of the planet, now that nuclear power is snaking its way slowly and surely through every major nation, but also that their lives will be directly threatened by this group of separatists."

Eisenhower knew about these powerful men of "The Brotherhood". He knew their names. Or most of them, at least. They wielded so much power, so much financial leverage, that they were untouchable to even himself, the President of the United States! They were important people and unashamedly occupied the top of the Earth's pedestal. They were quiet, smart, and kept just in the periphery of the public's eye. Only a handful of politicians knew *some* of those involved in this "*Brotherhood*". Otherwise, their operations and interests were held out of reach of even the more powerful hands in the world. Eisenhower knew enough of the operations among them. They knew of things otherworldly. They supposedly understood *real* human and world history. They had the knowledge of pure truth. And once he understood this, he thirsted for the same luxuries. He wanted to be walking alongside those in the "elevated" world, no longer beside the people that lived in the makeshift realm that was created for them by the elites.

Across a coffee table from him, sat two individuals that knew everything that there was worth knowing. The power that they had was still more than he could fathom. It made him green. Green like the floral curtains shading the gathering room. He felt the chair beneath himself, made of pine wood and leather. It was shrinking and becoming unsteady on the ground. He planted his feet, bracing himself to keep from falling over as his mind swirled, fearing that somehow, without moving, one of these men pulled a leg of pine from underneath him. His skin crawled at the idea that Elder, a thoroughly corrupt political rival, was capable of having more power than himself. The essence of evil he felt throughout the entirety of this meeting was circling the room, like a faint shadow that only the fearing man could see. This evil was their weapon. It came with them everywhere they went, like a hellhound on a leash. Its fangs of death and breath of misery were right in front of his face.

He chose his words carefully, yet eagerly:

"What can I do to help...?" Eisenhower said, trying to appease the beast.

Edler's slimy smirk returned. "What you can do, Mr. President, is make a strong case to our few remaining allies that this whole ordeal is similar to that of the past war's conflict in Europe. But rather than a conflict between fascists and communists, this battle will be that of communists and capitalists. Or fascism versus democracy. However you want to spin it. Personally, Americans are real up in arms about Marxism these days."

The President raised an eyebrow. "Marxism? Communism? The people of America and most of the world are already against that. McCarthyism is already supported by many. There isn't a need to use it for leverage against Mai-Xeng. He won't care."

"It won't matter what he says or thinks about it. He'll tell his allies his side. But we need to tell *our* allies that Marxism is a greater threat to democracy and the free world than they know. And that Mai-Xeng plans to institute it in plans to rival capitalism, threatening the western way of life. He may even bring the Soviets into the conflict, at this rate. Maybe remind the people who the Bolsheviks were, and how communism turned out for that governed population."

Eisenhower scoffed. "That McCarthy is a nut. And you want

to give him a brighter spotlight?"

"You don't have to defend his beliefs. You can denounce them if you'd like. But turn his words into your own and convince the public that China is gathering nations to deploy an enormous Marxist agenda for a third of the world. Even better, convince yourself of this *new truth*. It will help you sleep, maybe even improve your golf game." Elder sipped his tea again, peering over the glass like a crocodile does at the water's surface, eyeing its prey, waiting patiently to coax it closer to its jaws before the final blow is delivered. The evil became a tornado in the room, turning man into beast. The crocodile continued. "We don't want another World War. But we need to keep this transfer of power limited and in our reach. If we let Mai-Xeng get too far into his plan, whatever it may be, it will become harder for us to secure the safety of the globe. Wouldn't you say, Mr. President, that communism indeed must be extinguished?" He asked this like a true politician, playing a game of pretend just to pull you closer and closer to his razor-sharp teeth.

Eisenhower hesitated as time slowed to a crawl. The Shadow Man, who never even sipped his coffee, stared intently at him with unblinking, hungry, predatory eyes. Eisenhower thought it best to move these two men along, pushing away their evil presence as fast as he could.

He nodded. "Keep in touch with my people. We'll do what we can to cut those Asian Commies at the root." Then, a smile appeared beneath his nose and over clenched teeth.

"Thank you again, Mr. President..."

"You can call me Dwight," he responded. Standing up, he reached his hand across to shake his guests' hands. Only Elder accepted the gesture and shook. His smile was electric, as his crocodile snout closed around Eisenhower's outstretched arm, pulling him under the swamp's surface where he could finish his prey.

"You'll hear from us soon, don't you worry," is all Elder said as the two men got up and left the premises of Camp David, leaving Eisenhower wading in his sweat-filled socks on an uneven chair.

———

Elder sat five hundred feet above ground, next to his mysterious associate, in the helicopter leaving Camp David.

"We need to help France maintain territory in South Vietnam," said Elder. The Shadow Man nodded once. "With the U.S. playing along with us, we'll be able to keep the upper-hand on Mai-Xeng. Keep the resources flowing towards our territory."

In a deep, raspy German voice, the Shadow Man said, "We don't like France being there."

"It will only be for a short time, just until we figure out a way to keep *everything* together."

The associate shook his head slowly, menacingly. "*We...do not like...France.*"

"What do you like, then?" Even Elder was getting unnerved now.

"We want the U.S. on the ground. We want nothing to do with France."

"That will never happen. No matter how much we propagandize the military and people. That will undoubtedly start something too large in scale to keep under control."

"We want Vietnam, Laos, and Cambodia. We need to stay as close to Mai-Xeng as possible without going into China."

"Getting our troops there won't happen. Not a lot of them, at least. South Vietnam doesn't like the French being there. What makes you think a bigger force will be any different?"

"The French presence has muddied the water there. We think finding a new Vietnamese President will benefit us instantly, giving us time to slowly bleed in the American intelligence as needed."

Elder cocked his head. "Silent coup?"

Slowly the associate nodded. "There's a project we've been working on abroad. We weren't sure we'd have much use for it, but this feud will be the perfect first trial."

"What project is it?"

"A project that will separate us from our necessary and purposeful actions."

Elder shook his head. "What does that mean?"

The Shadow Man stared at him with his blank, black eyes. Two voids that were deeper than space itself, and possibly more soulless. Elder pivoted the conversation back to the "need-to-know".

"Even if the Agency succeeds at a silent coup, what would putting troops on the ground do for us?"

"Protect our new President, while slowly infiltrating other nations of interest, then taking all of Vietnam when the timing is right. We need American firepower and strategy."

Edler nodded. "Get as close to the enemy as we can, then find a way to topple them once the clock strikes midnight."

"It will be a long, bloody game of cat and mouse."

"Well, war makes for great economies. What American can argue against a flourishing economy? And I'm sure our Brothers will appreciate the industry that is sure to come. I say, the bloodier the better!"

The Shadow Man remained emotionless. The remainder of the helicopter ride was silent as they flew south towards Washington.

Part 3

<u>Sentenced To Burn</u>

Fall 1954

Luzon, Philippines

NOT EVEN THE COASTAL BREEZE COULD KEEP HIM COOL ENOUGH TO FIGHT THE SWEAT SOAKING HIS BODY. A mugginess as thick as velvet curtains hung in the air. Senator Adam Elder had turned his white button-down shirt to a subtle grey under the armpits already, and he'd only been grounded for ten minutes. As steamy and hot as the day was, he couldn't help but feel as if he were still on vacation. The tropical entry to the island of Luzon had introduced new excitement to this business venture he was already anxious for. After flying by plane from California to Manilla, then jumping into his favorite form of travel (helicopter), it was an adventure into the hidden hills of the northern Philippines island where he got to see beautiful landscapes that had no equal in his lifetime. It was his first trip to any part of Asia, and best of all, it was an all-expenses paid trip.

He wished it wouldn't be over after only a single day, but that was the only downside to this mission he helped procure. Standing under a thatch canopy and smoking a cigar, he removed his sunglasses to admire the unique hills of Luzon. Stone formations that looked like steps for creatures larger than man, ascending and descending into the terrain in an oddly natural way. "*Waterfalls of terra,*" he thought. "*Oh, how nature intrigues me, never leaving me completely satisfied.*" He pulled a pocket watch from his khaki-brown slacks. "*Landed fifteen minutes ago and still haven't received a welcome.*"

Next to the thatch canopy was a short stairwell that descended six feet into the ground and was eventually disrupted by a steel door. A building could not be observed above ground, and neither was a handle, latch, or knob to the door. So he was forced to wait outside and enjoy the last bit of tobacco in his cigar. The heli-pilot that brought him here was keeping an eye on him from the side of the aircraft. "*Little fucker's got no idea who I am.*" The pilot was supposedly an American Operative specifically based for this site that Elder was now visiting. But he hadn't liked the kid's attitude the entire flight up from the capital, ignoring the two questions Elder had asked him about this site's progress.

"Your eyes stuck or something?" Elder barked at the pilot. "Look somewhere else, prick!"

Slowly, the young pilot turned his head towards the forest surrounding them. Just as he did so, the steel door slammed open, and emerging from the underground stairwell was a gentleman wearing a military green button-up and khaki slacks as well. Older than Elder, this man with short white combed-over hair waved him over to the stairwell.

This was the man Elder had travelled to see; Agent Avery Strickland. For being the head of this site's operation, he came off incredibly paranoid, at least to Elder. Out of pettiness, Elder took his time to amble over to the stairwell while he sucked on the already finished cigar.

"Fifteen minutes, Strickland," Elder said with annoyance in his voice. "*Fifteen minutes* I stood out there and had that bastard pilot glaring me down."

"Apologies, Senator," said Strickland. He had as smooth a

voice as Elder. "We don't get many visitors. Especially ones leaving the same day." He let out a quick nervous laugh as he held open the steel door in the stairwell hole. "After you, Senator."

Behind the door was a completely dirt hallway, with gas lamps lining the walls on connecting fixtures. As soon as the door behind them had closed, Strickland relaxed as they made their way down the damp, dirty tunnel.

"Probably wasn't expecting to be visiting a foxhole today, huh?" He chuckled again, smiling confidently at Elder. Elder found it odd how light-hearted this character was for being around something he considered no-laughing-matter. But then again, optimism and positivity were likely necessary to keep sane down here.

They walked through the tunnel until another dirt-lain set of stairs led down to a second door. This time, it opened to reveal a tiled walkway with very comfortable lighting. It was like they had stepped into the nicest hospital on the planet. Perfectly constructed in the ground and hidden, the corridor smelled as refreshing as the tropical air outside and anything but stale. Not far along the hallway, two men waited for them, dressed in green uniforms and brandishing miniature machine guns that hung from straps around their necks.

"We know who you are," Strickland said to Elder, "but it's protocol to search any new arrival. They'll be quick and gentle."

Elder sighed, but he understood. This wasn't the first time he'd gone through pat downs, and it won't be nearly his last. After he was groped softly by the guards, Elder followed his host down the hallway. The two guards trailed closely behind them.

"Are these goons going to be following us around all day?" Elder asked.

"Agent Farabie and Agent Douglas," Strickland said in a

serious tone this time. "They are highly trained and part of our Special Operations Unit. They know everything there is to know about this place, and I don't suggest upsetting either of them with comments such as that one."

Elder made a face, mocking his host. Because Elder was young for a politician and still in good shape, he had an ego that followed him everywhere. And he welcomed it to most places.

Beautiful landscape artwork of the Philippine countryside lined the walls, attempting to create the illusion that you were above ground enjoying the real scenery. It was oddly soothing to Elder, and it gently lulled him as he admired every detailed inch. Green foliage, light blue skies, flowers of every color imaginable.

"Who decorated these walls?" Edler had to know.

"We've got some pretty talented people at this site, Senator," replied Strickland. "You'd be amazed at the skills some of these killers conceal." He allowed another friendly smile to his face. "Farabie behind you contributed to a lot of it, actually."

Elder turned around and nodded his head in approval to the stern soldier at his back. "What a wonderful gift you have," he added with a hint of mockery and a smirk. Farabie maintained his stoney expression. Turning his attention back to Strickland, Elder asked, "How's progress down here?"

"Depends on what part of the project you're asking about," replied Strickland.

"All of it."

Strickland sighed. "Well, the basics come down to promising results in one, and outstanding results in the other. That's why I ask."

"Okay, tell me what's wrong with the former."

Elder's bluntness and displeasure was beginning to annoy all three agents. Strickland continued, "Nothing is wrong. But with Project Birdsong, we're dealing with intelligent individuals that for long periods are disobedient. Conditioning them takes extra time, and sometimes it isn't worth our time. We've had the most setbacks within this specific project. However, we're less than a year from graduating a perfect specimen." They came upon a window that peered into a small auditorium. Eight bald men in blue jumpsuits sat watching a large television screen placed on a table at the front of the room, seated in wooden desks that you would normally see in a school. All of them appeared younger than Elder, closer in age to the armed agents behind him. They sat handcuffed to their chairs. Two Agents dressed similarly to Farabie and Douglas stood at the front of the group, armed with the same firepower. They watched the blue jumpsuits closely. Strickland continued, "Notice how the television is not turned on? Yet, they stare at it as if Jesus is talking to them from it."

Elder knew what the goal of this experiment was, but he wasn't sure the process it would take to get there. "Is this some sort of exercise?"

"Precisely. Though this exercise is quite brief, it is effective. We are using intense blue light testing on this group. When exposed to direct and elongated light this low on the color spectrum, it messes with the receptors in the eyes, from what we've found. Furthermore, when you mess with the eyes, you mess with the brain and—oh good, they're about to begin."

Just then, the lights cut out in the room, then a bright red bullseye appeared on the television. For ten seconds this lasted, before the television flickered an irritating signal of bright white and blue flashes. At the end of the flashing, the television turned off and the lights in the room returned. All the men in jumpsuits had their heads cocked to a side; four to the left, four to the right.

"These men are very hard to train," said Strickland. "We call them '*Shepards*'. As disobedient as you'd expect from imprisoned enemy agents, these fuckers take months to break before they learn to cooperate. Hell, they don't even learn. They don't operate under their own brain power as they near the end of their conditioning."

"So, you wear them down completely? Like breaking a horse?"

Strickland sat with that question as he considered. "Yeah. Kind of like that. The goal is to change everything we don't like in these killers to admirable traits. Theoretically, we believe we can alter their memories, or replace them, so that they can't remember who they are or where they're from. And then we change their futures by taking advantage of those gaps in their memory. It's been discovered that people without a memory of their past personality or personal history are much easier to control."

"And this is the former, which you considered 'promising', correct?" asked Elder

"Yes. Promising is sort of an understatement for what we have done with Birdsong. We've had a few Shepards make it to the field for testing."

"And?"

Strickland smiled. "Let me show you the rest of what we've been cooking, first."

Elder and Strickland were seated at a narrow window that offered a view of a small cinema-like theater. Several rows, each one resting lower than the previous, descending to a stage with a large, flat, blank screen. The lights were dimmed inside the theater, as the two spectators awaited the specimen. The bunker complex they were in was quite large, surprisingly to Elder. After they had left the showing of the so-called "Shepards", they descended further into the subterranean compound by elevator. Three floors deeper into the earth, inside a steel box with six buttons indicating different levels of the bunker. It wasn't unusual for the CIA to build something so impressive in such an atypical and inconvenient location.

"As you know," said Elder, "we have taken a great liking to the projects your Agency has undergone over the past several years. Your unorthodox experiments are what have made you stand out above the rest."

"Thank you, Senator," replied Strickland. "We at the CIA believe there is untapped human potential to be discovered and harnessed. And the more we understand about ourselves, the more advanced our society can become."

"That's all fine for the newspapers, but we want you to continue your research into the *supernatural* findings, as well. Not just this 'human potential' shit."

"Senator, with all due respect, I think you are underestimating our influence within the Agency. What you are insinuating about us is that we are only working simply within the realm of reality. But the box you think we are working inside of is purposefully made to appear small and simple. However, from the public's perspective, they cannot imagine what is inside the box. And even if they could, they'd be in *your* position; sitting next to me with no ability to truly navigate the labyrinth of misdirection that keeps our—how some may say…*controversial* experiments hidden and safe with only us and our serious investors." Strickland was slowly growing more irritated with this politician as the seconds passed.

"I'm no stranger to any of this."

Strickland cleared his throat. "Senator, these 'supernatural' aspects are being researched. We have entered a new age of technology and thought that is bringing us to brand new understandings of what it means to live and breathe. Think of Project Birdsong as a tree. Inside this facility, we are the foundation of this Project. And around other parts of the world are our branches that have grown directly from this facility. And much like trees, there are many, many more than just one in the world. This Project is one of many trees being grown by the CIA, Senator. An entire forest is budding, and progress in every aspect of life is being unveiled every passing minute by our Agency." Strickland checked his watch impatiently. "You ever hear anything about *Project Z*? Over in the States? 1940's, New Mexico area, I think."

"Of course. Several peers of mine were invested in that project. Didn't go anywhere though, after a couple of years."

"It was intended to protect important leaders and people from radiation poisoning, following an expected blast. But it was rumored to also add further protection from viruses and even aging."

"Yes. Odd stuff, if you ask me. Unrealistic."

"Yes, but the *right* kind of odd stuff. And *very* realistic these days. *Project Z* ended in a major FBI investigation that also went nowhere. Good on your guys' part to cut ties. I don't believe anyone was arrested after all that. What a bloody mess it was. And a lot of people there at El Loto went missing. Dozens. Never found. And not a shred of proof that anything was ever done. Which makes me think—anyways, I think those guys had an intriguing idea over there. Really matches the ideals of your people up top."

Elder nodded slowly, keeping his eyes on Strickland as he spoke again.

"What I'm getting at is, there are odd experiments going on everywhere. Any psychopath that can get a hold of some fancy technology and some funding can poke and prod his way through the most demented of experiments. The El Loto Massacre is a prime example of poor handling and mismanaged oversight. Here, at the CIA, we have all the best tech, tools, people, funding, ideas, investors, and allies. We will always give you the best results, with your best interests as a priority because we share similar agendas." A man in a white jumpsuit was dragged into the theater by a pair of Agents and was placed in the front row of seats facing the large screen. He was limp and unresistant. "You want supernatural? We have that. But not here. What we have, is the *Ultra-natural*." Strickland put his index finger to the glass, pointing down to the man sitting in the front row. "*L...S...D*, Senator. A hallucinogen that seemingly transports you to another dimension, unlocking Ultra-human abilities. Our team believes it can be weaponized once ingested by an individual, then conditioned to use it. And this particular individual is what we call a *Joe*."

The large screen turned on and the lights in the room cut out. The screen flashed images and fast cuts of short cinema that churned even Elder's stomach into a knot. He wasn't quite sure what he was watching, but he broke into a greasy sweat watching the intense images that pounded his brain with the intensity of a physical fist. He could hear the faintest of words echoing through the theater every few seconds. One word at a time that vibrated through the theater.

"Without this glass," said Strickland, "you'd be forced to protect your ears from that voice. It's so low in frequency that it's reaching a deeper part of the brain with its vibrations. The words we've scripted out to our reader are being imprinted onto our *Joe* down there."

Elder looked down at the man in the white jumper. He was sitting perched upright, keeping his hands comfortably at the sides of his chair. Only his head was wavering subtly back and forth atop his neck as he was entranced by the screen.

"Is this not damaging his ears?" Elder asked.

Strickland shook his head. "Not in the slightest. He's become fond of it now, actually. This late in the process, it's pleasing for him to experience all this over and over again, day to day."

"How is this pleasing to anybody? This is torture."

Strickland laughed. "Exactly. It is *fucking* torture. That man down there we call MK-Beagle. He's the only functioning Joe we currently have. And he's by far the most promising we've had."

Elder watched as MK-Beagle sat very still. "If *he's* functioning, what's considered not?"

"The *Over-Fried*, we say." Strickland chuckled. "We have most of those still here on IV's, studying the late effects and overdose qualities they developed from the drugs. Some we dumped back onto the streets early on because we needed more space and, honestly, didn't want them around anymore."

"Tell me more…" Elder was enthralled by the images. Never had he seen colors on a silver screen. Intense, vibrant colors that were flooding his brain. The Agency always proved that they were ahead of the rest, possessing technology that the public won't be introduced to for over a decade. Without a doubt, the CIA was even ahead of all other intelligence by a couple years.

It was beautiful. Explosions flashed for a second, then you were looking at a direct contrast of a beautiful red flower, then the insides of a human man, to the pure naked flesh of a human woman, to a hurricane of vibrant spiraling colors, to pulsing shades of grey, to animated cartoons, to a man and woman laying together in pleasure, to a gun firing towards the screen, to a tank rolling over trenches, to glass shattering, to Jesus, to Satan, to fields of clover, to men lit on fire, to sex, to blood, to war, to beauty, to sex, to blood, sex, war, heaven, blood.

"He's hallucinating off of our homemade Acids," said

Strickland. "LCD, MDMA, Mescaline, and other forms of hypnotics. Paired with his melancholy and pre-diagnosed schizophrenia, his brain was that much easier for us to tap into and change. When dealing with Joes, it's been easiest to mold a breaking mind. A sick one, if you must. We know we can extract information through the use of other such extreme drugs, so here we wanted to push further into opening other parts of the mind. As you saw back there with our *Shepards*, the goal is to *close* their minds so that we can assume full control over them—"

"Control?" Elder said quietly, still sweating, unable to divert his eyes from the captivating film.

"Mind-control. The Shepards are being altered in every way mentally so they can never become a threat to us again. They will become our pets. But Beagle down there has a different purpose. Half the time, he is withdrawing from the drugs he's being forced to take." Strickland grinned. "He is conscious, though, that something we are giving him makes the voices and demons go away. But whatever else is inside him is inviting them back in."

"It's magnificent," said Elder.

"The other parts of his day are filled with highs that allow us to open neurological pathways. Training him in such ways that he can only act when in a certain state. That state we call '*Activated*'. What you would never guess is that that man down there is almost as dangerous as those highly trained killers back in the other room. And this *bozo* was just some loaf we pulled out of the discharge pile of the Army."

"What'd he do to get discharged?"

The Agent laughed again. "Performed terribly at everything he did. Became a danger to others around him for how incompetent he was. He ended up shooting his Staff Seargent in the foot by accident. Now, after a somewhat lengthy balancing act of opening and closing parts of his neurological system, he's nearly obedient at every level upon hearing a string of carefully read words in perfect order. Concurrently, the killer within is 'Activated'. And soon, he'll be to level eleven, where he will be able to move in and out of this hypnosis by the sound of only his Shepard's voice."

Elder felt a tear roll over his cheek. The first tear in years, and he couldn't attach any specific emotion to it. "What are these images for, then? How—the colors…" His emotions were hardly in check.

"Just another exercise to help dig into that feeble little brain of his. All his emotions are being thrown into a melting pot so he will eventually be unable to think or feel anything while under our hypnosis. The words being spoken all around him are building the personality we desire of him while spellbound."

"Imagine this power you've created," said Elder softly as he began to understand it all, "but on a scale so large that you could control your enemies through psychological warfare. Through years of mental conditioning, you could keep anyone and everyone circling in the palm of your hand…"

"And they would never think of leaving it." Strickland turned to Elder. "So, do we have a deal?"

Elder thought for a few seconds. "You tested in the field, you said?"

"Oh yes. Several times."

"And the results were…?"

"All partial."

Elder turned to face Strickland for the first time in what seemed like hours. "Explain 'partial'."

"We ran our best specimen over to a friend of ours in Louisiana. He's thrown some of his money towards the CIA in other interested experiments and we heard he needed some help in his business."

"What business?"

"Well, I'm sure you won't judge our decision, but he may or may not be a trusted head of the Dixie Mafia down there in the south. And he's been losing quite a few men to a recent crackdown on organized crime. Specifically in his Alabama territory. He needed this new Attorney General gone, and we offered our assistance."

Elder nodded. "I know about the assassination. Helped me out with some ties I got down there. That was this Project? Birdsong?"

"Yes." Strickland was beaming.

"They found the killer, though."

"Hence, the partial success. Our Joe was captured. But our Shepard got away."

"So, the Shepard is there to activate, then deactivate the—"

"And to assist in the job as well. But it is more important that the Shepard returns to us, so they work from the shadows of the operation. The Joes can be replaced by anybody. Shepards are harder to come by."

"So, you got your Shepard back, at least."

"Well, actually no." Strickland sighed. "We lost track of him shortly after he deactivated his Joe."

Elder's eyes widened. "What the hell does that mean? Is that going to endanger this project in anyway?"

"Heavens no. The Joe's brain is a stew after reverting to *Protocol C*, which our Shepard successfully initiated. And the Shepard is still under our control. He just—is missing. He might never turn up, but he isn't a threat to us. He might go and get himself caught after a short-circuit up top eventually, but we've protected ourselves very well during the exercises. Like I said, they have no memory of their past."

Elder sat back and relaxed as the theater lights turned up

slowly. The film was over, and the booming voice had concluded.

"Senator, I present to you, the masterpiece we call Project Birdsong."

Part 4

The Disloyal

Spring 1961

New York City, New York

PRESIDENT JOHN F. KENNEDY TAKES THE PODIUM. Dozens of political figures and press associates stand clapping to his left and to his right. A crowd of a couple hundred editors, publishers, and others employed by the press return to their seated positions as the thundering applause comes to a halt. The cameras roll, ready to capture the President's speech to the American Newspaper Publishers Association.

"Mr. Chairman. Ladies and gentlemen. I appreciate very much your generous invitation to be here tonight. You bear heavy responsibilities these days and an article I read some time ago reminded me of how particularly heavily the burdens of present day events bear upon your profession. You may remember that in 1851 the New York Herald Tribune under the sponsorship and publishing of Horace Greeley, employed as its London correspondent an obscure journalist by the name of Karl Marx. We are told that foreign correspondent Marx, stone broke, and with a family ill and undernourished, constantly appealed to Greeley and managing editor Charles Dana for an increase in his munificent salary of $5 per installment, a salary which he and Engels ungratefully labeled as the 'lousiest petty bourgeois cheating'. But when all his financial appeals were refused, Marx looked around for other means of livelihood and fame, eventually terminating his relationship with the tribune and devoting his talents full time to the cause that would bequeath the world the seeds of Leninism, Stalinism, revolution and the Cold War. If only this capitalistic New York newspaper had treated him more kindly; if only Marx had remained a foreign correspondent, history might have been different. And I hope all publishers will bear this lesson in mind the next time they receive a poverty-stricken appeal for the small increase in the expense account from an obscure newspaper man. I have selected as the title of my remarks tonight 'The President and the Press'. Some may suggest that this would be more naturally worded 'The President Versus the Press'. But those are not my sentiments tonight. It is true, however, that when a well-known diplomat from another country demanded recently that our State Department repudiate certain newspaper attacks on his colleagues it was unnecessary for us to reply that this Administration was not responsible for the press, for the press had already made it clear that it was not responsible for this administration. Nevertheless, my purpose here tonight is not to deliver the usual assault on the so-called one-party press. On the contrary, in recent months I have rarely heard any complaints about political bias in the press except from a few Republicans. Nor is it my purpose tonight to discuss or defend the televising of Presidential Press Conferences. I think it is highly beneficial to have some twenty-million Americans regularly sit in on these conferences to observe, if I may so, the incisive, the intelligent and the courteous qualities displayed by your Washington correspondents. Nor, finally, are these remarks intended to examine the proper degree of privacy which the press should allow to any President and his family. If in the last few months your White House reporters and photographers have been attending church services with regularity, that has surely done them no harm. On the other hand, I realize that your staff and wire service photographers may be complaining that they do not enjoy the same green privileges at the local golf courses that they once did. It is true that my predecessor did not object as I do to pictures of one's golfing skill in action. But neither on the other hand did he ever bean a Secret Service man. My topic tonight is a more sober of one concern to publishers, as well as editors. I want to talk about our common responsibilities in the face of a common danger. The events of recent weeks may have helped illuminate that challenge for some; but the dimensions of its threat have loomed large on the horizon for many years. Whatever our hopes may be for the future—for reducing this threat or living in it—there is no escaping either the gravity or the totality of its challenge to our survival and to our security—a challenge that confronts us in unaccustomed ways in every sphere of human activity. This deadly challenge imposes upon our society two requirements of direct concern both to the press and to the President—two requirements that seem almost contradictory in tone, but which must be reconciled and fulfilled if we are to meet this national peril. I refer, first, to the need for a far greater public information; and, second, to the need for far greater official secrecy.

"The very word 'secrecy' is repugnant in a free and open society, and we are as a people inherently and historically opposed to secret societies, to secret oaths and to secret proceedings. We decided long ago that the dangers of excessive and unwarranted concealment of pertinent facts far outweighed the dangers which are cited to justify it. Even today, there is little value in opposing the threat of a closed society by imitating its arbitrary restrictions. Even today, there is little value in ensuring the survival of our nation if our traditions do not survive with it. And there is very grave danger that an announced need for increased security will be seized upon by those anxious to expand its meaning to the very limits of official censorship and concealment. That I do not intend to permit to the extent that is in my control. And no official of my Administration, whether his rank is high or low, civilian or military, should interpret my words here tonight as an excuse to censor the news, to stifle dissent, to cover up our mistakes or to withhold from the press and the public the facts they deserve to know. But I do ask every publisher, every editor, and every newsman in the nation to reexamine his own standards, and to recognize the nature of our country's peril. In time of war, the government and the press have customarily joined in an effort based largely on self-discipline, to prevent unauthorized disclosures to the enemy. In time of 'clear and present danger', the courts have held that even the privileged rights of the First Amendment must yield to the public's need for national security. Today no war has been declared—and however fierce the struggle may be, it may never be declared in the traditional fashion. Our way of life is under attack. Those who make themselves our enemy are advancing around the globe. The survival of our friends is in danger. And yet no war has been declared, no borders have been crossed by marching troops, no missiles have been fired. If the press is awaiting a declaration of war before it imposes the self-discipline of combat conditions, then I can only say that no war ever posed a greater threat to our society. If you are awaiting a finding of 'clear and present danger', then I can only say that the danger has never been more clear and its presence has never been more imminent. It requires a change in outlook, a change in tactics, a change in missions—by the government, by the people, by every businessman or labor leader, and by every newspaper. For we are opposed around the world by a monolithic and ruthless conspiracy that relies primarily on covert means for expanding its sphere of influence—on infiltration instead of invasion, on subversion instead of elections, on intimidation instead of free choice, on guerrillas by night instead of armies by day. It is a system which has conscripted vast human and material resources into the building of a tightly knit, highly efficient machine that combines military, diplomatic, intelligence, economic, scientific and political operations. Its preparations are concealed, not published. Its mistakes are buried, not headlined. Its dissenters are silenced, not praised. No expenditure is questioned, no rumor is printed, no secret is revealed. It conducts the Cold War, in short, with a wartime discipline no democracy would ever hope or wish to match. Nevertheless, every democracy recognizes the necessary restraints of national security—and the question remains whether those restraints need to be more strictly observed if we are to oppose this kind of attack as well as outright invasion. For the facts of the matter are that this nation's foes have openly boasted of acquiring through our newspapers information they would otherwise hire agents to acquire through theft, bribery or espionage, that details of this nation's covert operations have been available to every newspaper reader, friend and foe alike; that the size, the strength, the location and the nature of our forces and weapons, and our plans and strategy for our use, have all been pinpointed in the press and other news media to a degree sufficient to satisfy any foreign power; and that, in at least one case, the publication of details concerning a secret mechanism whereby satellites were followed required its alteration at the expense of considerable time and money. The newspapers which printed these stories were loyal, patriotic, responsible and well-meaning. Had we been engaged in open warfare, they undoubtedly would not have published such items. But in the absence of open warfare, they recognized only the tests of journalism and not the tests of national security. And my question tonight is whether additional tests should not now be adopted. The question is for you alone to answer. No public official should answer it for you. No governmental plan should impose its restraints against your will. But I would be failing in my duty to the nation, in considering all of the responsibilities that we now bear and all of the means at hand to meet those responsibilities, if I did not commend this problem to your attention, and urge its thoughtful consideration. On many earlier occasions, I have said—and your newspapers have constantly said—that these are times that appeal to every citizen's sense of sacrifice and self-discipline. They call out to every citizen to weigh his rights and comforts against his obligations to the common good. I cannot now believe that those citizens who serve in the newspaper business consider themselves exempt from that appeal. I have no intention of establishing a new Office of War Information to govern the flow of news. I am not suggesting any new forms of censorship or any new types of security classifications. I have no easy answer to the dilemma that I have posed, and would not seek to impose it if I had one. But I am asking the members of the newspaper profession and the industry in this country to reexamine their own responsibilities, to consider the degree and the nature of the present danger, and to heed the duty of self-restraint which that danger imposes upon us all. Every newspaper now asks itself, with respect to every story: 'Is it news?' All I suggest is that you add the question: 'Is it in the interest of the national security?' And I hope that every group in America—unions and businessmen and public officials at every level—will ask the same question of their endeavors, and subject their actions to the same exacting tests. And should the press of America consider and recommend the voluntary assumption of specific new steps or machinery, I can assure you that we will cooperate whole-heartedly with those recommendations. Perhaps there will be no recommendations. Perhaps there is no answer to the dilemma faced by a free and open society in a cold and secret war. In times of peace, any discussion of this subject, and any action that results, are both painful and without precedent. But this is a time of peace and peril which knows no precedent in history.

"It is the unprecedented nature of this challenge that also gives rise to your second obligation—an obligation which I share. And that is our obligation to inform and alert the American people —to make certain that they possess all the facts that they need, and understand them as well—the perils, the prospects, the purposes of our program and the choices that we face. No President should fear public scrutiny of his program. For from that scrutiny comes understanding; and from that understanding comes support or opposition. And both are necessary. I am not asking your newspapers to support the Administration, but I am asking your help in the tremendous task of informing and alerting the American people. For I have complete confidence in the response and dedication of our citizens whenever they are fully informed. I not only could not stifle controversy amongst your readers—I welcome it. This Administration intends to be candid about its errors; for as a wise man once said: 'An error does not become a mistake until you refuse to correct it.' We intend to accept full responsibility for our errors; and we expect you to point them out when we miss them. Without debate, without criticism, no Administration and no country can succeed—and no republic can survive. That is why the Athenian lawmaker Solon decreed it a crime for any citizen to shrink from controversy. And that is why our press was protected by the First Amendment—the only business in America specifically protected by the Constitution—not primarily to amuse and entertain, not to emphasize the trivial and the sentimental, not to simply 'give the public what it wants'—but to inform, to arouse, to reflect, to state our dangers and our opportunities, to indicate our crises and our choices, to lead, mold, educate and sometimes even anger public opinion. This means greater coverage and analysis of international news—for it is no longer far away and foreign but close at hand and local. It means greater attention to improved understanding of the news as well as improved transmission. And it means, finally, that government at all levels, must meet its obligation to provide you with the fullest possible information outside the narrowest limits of national security—and we intend to do it.

"It was early in the Seventeenth Century that Francis Bacon remarked on three recent inventions already transforming the world: the compass, gunpowder and the printing press. Now the links between the nations first forged by the compass have made us all citizens of the world, the hopes and threats of one becoming the hopes and threats of us all. In that one world's effort to live together; the evolution of gunpowder to its ultimate limit has warned mankind of the terrible consequences of failure. And so it is to the printing press—to the recorder of man's deeds, the keeper of his conscience, the courier of his news—that we look for strength and assistance, confident that with your help man will be what he was born to be: free and independent."

-President John F. Kennedy
Address before the
American Newspaper Publishers Association
Waldorf-Astoria Hotel
April 27, 1961

A stewardess placed the red blended cocktail on the table beside the most powerful man in the world. The President of The United States of America enjoyed liquor with quite a bit of sweet in it. Frozen, blended, not too strong, and full of flavor. John F. Kennedy was not paying attention to the woman who dropped off his drink. Instead, he was mulling over some documents his Secretary of State, Dean Rusk, had handed him the moment he stepped on the plane.

It was only yesterday he delivered his incredibly direct yet cryptic speech to the American Newspaper Publishers Association (ANPA), and the people of The United States. With the tensions of the Cold War thickening the atmosphere of the world, national security was of the utmost concern. But not without protecting and informing the citizens within the nation. John believed something of a crisis regarding the people's rights and privacies was looming, and the press needed to help with keeping every person in the loop of truth. He was tired of the establishment media companies passing off this belief that it was best to just "give the people what they want", and to not think of the consequences stemming from such loose and foolhardy sentiments. As a business, John understood why they did it. If people want something in this society of capitalism, they can go out and buy it. Tabloids and entertainment sell more paper than do truth, doom, and gloom.

But this speech was meant to encourage the press and newspapers to be more unambiguous, honest, and forthright with the citizens of America. A time of distrust is on the horizon, along with an imminent war. Weighing Khrushchev and his threats, Cuba's unusual involvement at the moment, and the suspicious activities surrounding Vietnam, all put John Kennedy's social goals for his beloved country on hold. Instead of having the time or energy to build up his own nation's infrastructure and way of life, he was busy with meetings, debriefings, and negotiations. Anything and everything was happening that embodied stress for a President working to prevent a third World War in forty-five years. Because surely this would be the last, thanks to the impressively growing field of technological science. New weapons were being developed weekly by The States. Enemy spies prying into said technology were slowly becoming Code Yellow for this administration.

Espionage and infiltration. If the nukes weren't launched in the near future to destroy half the world, espionage and infiltration within the United States would crumble this nation faster than you can say "daquiri". The moment one enemy finds a way into American public office, more gaps are opened for more. Secrets of the nation, protecting the lives of all its citizens, become someone else's weapon to be used against it. He knew that moment had already arrived.

Hence the cryptic moments in his speech. John knows it's already too late to prevent the formal invasion and infiltration that has created a swamp in congress. The people began losing their rights without even knowing it, fifty years ago. The people of America, in John's eyes, needed to be informed that the capitalist-social structure of this country may benefit most within the nation, but created many enemies outside of it. What's terrifying and unknown by most is that the Americans are inching closer to the world others see fit for it.

These "others" are the aforementioned "secret societies". The first couple days after John took office, he was contacted by and introduced to some powerful men. These men, dressed to impress on the daily, were for the most part invisible to the public eye. Either having been seen or mentioned rarely or not at all. A couple of them he knew personally. Lord knows he was never friends with these elite members of society, but he'd been acquainted with them over the years as he began to gain favor from the public. Especially once he began his campaign trail. After these phone calls and surprise meetings, he felt unease that his whole life he may have been watched and tracked. These men would often mention old family members of his, previous schools he attended, old habits he most definitely had. Their words were working as a harbinger of future threats.

And John needed to know more about these men. So, just as every President over the past decade or so had experienced, he had sat in a room with some member of his cabinet he never remembers placing, and another pair of politicians with whom he had no affiliation. They told him, in the darkest, quietest room in the White House that there exist powers beyond the comprehension of even the most powerful man in the world, The United States President. Powers that pull every string without ever being seen. Powers that do what they want, when they need, where they're needed. But never will these powers make it obvious that they have fingerprints on any of their actions. They are unstoppable from the outside. And even if you find your way in, you're fighting shadows, ghosts. You may be able to form a picture of them, but not clear enough to separate them from any other ghastly thing. They, however, will haunt you every minute of your life until you get close enough to the stairs, where they will push you down, leaving you to suffer beneath the surface of the world you sought to protect.

John's eyes opened. He had dozed off in his leather backed chair while reading something in front of him. "*Agenda*", was at the top of the page he was holding. "*2 morning meetings tomorrow with 1) General Thompkins of the Pentagon, and 2) Interior decorator.*" He rubbed his eyes, reading that the last one again to be sure. "*Jackie's business, I suppose.*" His wife sure was obsessing over fashion and image even where the public couldn't access. But he knew the bedroom and hallways would be tasteful, at least.

He reached for his drink next to him and sipped, noticing that the slush of his cocktail had melted into a watered-down lame beverage. How long had he been out? The plane hadn't taken off. And his guest was still absent. He sat back in his chair and rubbed his forehead. The stress of it all was collapsing on him. Four hours of sleep a night over the past two years. All for the people of his country to prosper and live long happy lives. He had a plan to slowly and surely end the force that was preventing all that from happening. Yesterday's speech was the beginning of unraveling the evils for the people to see. "*One step at a time*".

His guest had arrived. The moment he had entered Air Force One the engine rumbled to life. It was late in the evening; the sun was just setting over the top of the concourse of New York International. Dark clouds began forming over the skyscrapers with some periodic flashes of lightning. John had instructed that the windows to the cabin remain uncovered as long as the sun was up. He stood to welcome his guest, reaching out with his hand to shake that of Senator Adam Elder of Louisiana. Elder had graying hair and a prominent mole on his left cheek that was noticeable from across most rooms. He appeared quite lively today, unlike the other few times John had met with him.

"Mr. President," Elder introduced himself with an obvious Louisiana accent.

"Senator," replied Kennedy. "Please, have a seat. Can I offer you a beverage?"

"No, thank you, sir." The two sat down across from another. The plane had already begun rolling across the tarmac. "I would enjoy peanuts or something salty. On second thought, maybe a glass of water, too." He smiled at Kennedy for an awkward moment.

"Of course." Kennedy pressed a button above his head and the stewardess immediately appeared behind him. "Water and something salty for Senator Elder, Clarice."

"As you wish, sir," the blonde beauty said with a sultry purr.

Kennedy stared at this man Elder for a moment, admiring his fashion and expensive-looking leather overcoat. He guessed it to be a Reid & Taylor or perhaps something bespoke imported from across the pond. Well-crafted and dashing, John could admit. He was regathering every bit of information he knew about Senator Elder that his Secretary of State, who was sitting in the other cabin, had recently briefed him on. And from the background known of Elder and the recent few calls John had taken since his speech, this was his first meeting of consequence.

"So, Senator," Kennedy started. He was calmer than he probably should have been. "I presume there is trouble brewing among some of your associates. I have had a great deal of calls coming from friends of yours, trying to coordinate some sort of gathering. I hope my aircraft will very much suffice as our conference room today."

"Of course, Mr. President," said Elder. "It's actually my first time getting to sit inside this beautiful vessel."

"Wonderful, isn't she?"

"Very, very impressive for something so big." He paused and cleared his throat. "Air Force One. Nothing more American than that, can't you agree?"

John put his hand up. Clarice returned with a water glass and a bowl of assorted salted snacks. She smiled and left the two politicians to their conversation. John's hand lowered.

"So, you received a call from a friend of mine," said Elder.

"That is right. More than one friend, more accurately."

"So, you must know that some of your words may have ruffled feathers?"

"I am aware."

"Not just any feathers, either sir. Feathers belonging to the largest birds to ever exist."

"Again, I am aware of my current situation…"

"I don't mean to stop you, John. But, I do. For the sake of sparing your breath."

John was mildly insulted by the use of his first name that revealed the low level of respect from this man he barely knew. The plane began to pick up speed, readying to ascend and arc back towards D.C. "Go on, then. Make your statements."

"You know of the Soviets involvement in Vietnam? Economically, they are stimulating Ho Chi Minh and his Northerners."

Kennedy stared blankly at this man, frustrated that he was being asked these inane questions by this patronizing boor.

"Well," Elder went on, "it would be detrimental to Western democracy if Communists began having each other's backs, wouldn't you agree?"

"Of course I would, Senator. But it isn't in my nation's best interests to interfere at this time. Hopefully, that call will never be answered."

"In all respects, Mr. President, you *did* place special forces and intelligence on the ground there."

"In the south, yes. They are there to observe and report. Nothing more."

Elder shook his head. "That's how it all starts, John." Kennedy flared his nostrils briefly at the use of his first name. "Our curiosity has brought influence directly into the conflict alongside the French. Once the Northerners or, worse, the Soviets or Chinese catch wind of your subversion, Vietnam will be shrouded in Napalm."

"There is no subversion occurring in the south, Adam." Elder smirked as his name was thrown into the stew of conversation. "The intelligence on the ground is instructed to not engage. We only need them there in the case of rapid escalation."

"Is that not what has happened over the past year? Rapid escalation?"

"Not to the level in which we need to sacrifice the lives of young Americans."

Elder chuckled, grabbing a handful of snack mix and sloppily forcing it into his mouth, crumbs rolling over himself and the carpet. With his mouth full, he said, "You don't know why the Agency is there, do you John? I think you hardly know how many Americans are planted there now."

Kennedy rubbed his chin, pinching his skin between his thumb and forefinger. "As President of the United States…"

"You don't." Elder interrupted. He stared at him, amused as he continued to chew his nuts.

"Enlighten me then, Adam. I don't enjoy these games politicians such as yourself play."

The tensions were escalating, as Kennedy assumed they would. This was the reason only the two sat in the cabin, away from either's people. This was a negotiation more than anything.

"1955, North Vietnam broke international law by refusing to retreat its militants in Vietnam, resulting in the South's refusal to participate in a unifying election. But, as you know, the Southerners were never actually a part of any of those accords that would 'unify' them. Had to do with the weakness and inefficiency of our allies over in France, let's say. As we came to discover shortly after, a major world leader may have been the reason this whole thing got kicked off over there. Someone bigger than Uncle Ho, and bigger than French occupation."

"You know who?" Kennedy asked.

"Of course I do."

"If you are unwilling to reveal this information to our government, I have no reason but to assume treason on your part, Senator."

"Oh, John," Elder smiled. He dipped the tips of his fingers in his water glass, cleaning them of the salt, and then wiping his lips. "You won't succeed in taking me out of the Senate, let alone taking away any of my connections. But I have more for you that, well, I think with your insatiable thirst for curiosity, you might enjoy and understand a little more. You see, in November of that same year, North Vietnam were surprisingly the ones that attacked first. The Viet Cong made their way down to the south, just east of the border of Cambodia, attacking the French occupants and their allies. Now, you would assume given the growing tension, we may have seen something major break out after the North revealed their hand."

"Invasion," is all Kennedy said.

Elder nodded. "Ho and the Northerners on their own with their lack of firepower, could not have had the guts to march straight south and begin attacking. Eisenhower, as you know, sent small sleeper groups to ensure Saigon had a backing. Between the Agency and the military, we could quietly counter what Ho Chi was hiding."

In a typical airplane, the storm growing beneath them would have kicked up a jet stream that would have caused a deal of turbulence. In this engineering marvel, they felt nothing from outside the plane. The turbulence was building within the luxurious cabin.

"He had allies way bigger than he should have for such a small nation's civil war," said Elder. His eyes and face were darker. He was hardly looking into the eyes of Kennedy anymore. "President Mai-Xeng of China has, as only people such as yourself and I know, been involved since Geneva. He has been pulling the strings since the day before all this shit hit the fan."

"Our intelligence hasn't proven that to be true."

Elder signaled to Kennedy with his wagging pointer finger.

"This is where things get cloudy for you, Mr. President. Have you considered all that you wrote in your speech? To me, you seemed confident that you knew everything. But," Elder smiled wide, "only the best magicians can fool even the rabbit. You are in such a place of power, and yet you know so little of a growing conflict."

"There's a silent war with the Soviets right now, Senator!" Kennedy thundered. "There are direct conflicts involving America that mean more than an Asian civil war. My job did not come with a crystal ball as you may think."

"I know it didn't, John. There are reasons for that. But I believe the Soviets have more involvement than we know. And part of what the Agency and our military are doing there is to ensure we don't lose Vietnam to the Communists."

Kennedy had had enough of the charade. He had lost his patience dealing with such a narcissistic politician. "I know who surrounds you. And I can begin to think of why such a small Eastern country has such a grasp on you and your alliances. I know of the Soviets stimulating the North with supplies. And I happen to know Khruschev was once, dare I say, a friend of yours and has since been lost. And I can think the same of a certain instigator you're terrified of."

Elder for the first time wavered in his demeanor of comfort. "Terrified is the opposite of what I am—"

"My apologies, Senator. I will not speak on your behalf, as you have mine. But I believe I am speaking for the ones that sent you here this evening. I could feel the tremors in their voices as they spoke to me on the phone."

"You know nothing! Not one damn thing!" Elder was beginning to raise his voice now.

"You heard my speech. And I think those breadcrumbs could be followed from far beyond the walls of that beautiful hotel."

"Whatever you're getting at, I believe you're misinformed, Mr. President."

Kennedy sat back and relaxed. He sipped at his daquiri which had all melted long ago. It too must have felt the heat in the cabin. "I never experienced hardship, Mr. Elder. Not until I took this position as a leader. I grew up privileged. A wealthy, caring family. An American family. I saw what the meaning of life, liberty, and the pursuit of happiness is truly about. Land of the free, Senator. It is our job as representatives to the people of the United States to uphold justice and liberties, ensuring equality for all. Soon, that will mean the *negroes* too. We are way past due in allowing them to join their fellow brothers in humanity, to live hand in hand, and as neighbors in a country that is now beginning to fight for what is right. My privileges, Senator, that I experienced growing up are what I wish and want for every man, woman, and child in this country. In the world. But first, the bricks must be placed, one at a time. And what better way to help our fellow Americans than to end the conspiracy you and your cult have put in action."

Elder was silent for a moment. Kennedy could see the man's darting eyes turning red, as he desperately tried to keep himself in check.

Kennedy continued. "I have seen things in Los Angeles that exposed me to your trickle-down elitist system. The power that comes with signing your life away to the devil. The sort of things that your everyday man find repugnant. Yes, Senator, I am overly curious. I believe I know what it means to challenge a complex system full of bankers, businessmen, and criminals. I know the consequences. But I have surrounded myself by the best people, that share my intentions, my beliefs, my cautions, certain that we can first save this country from your perilous grasp, and eventually the world. Slowly, we will drag you to the stage, in front of everyone—"

"The balance of the world is teetering on a cliff, Mr. President!" Elder snapped. Sweat was glistening on his forehead, and he was chewing his lower lip. He took a deep breath to calm himself momentarily. "Let me tell you a little truth, sir. I did not grow up with privilege. I lost my father to the First War. I experienced the Great Depression firsthand when I was just a young man. I saw a part of this country that is not filled with happiness or any pursuit of it. It's full of poverty, crime, murder. And all of it brought me to Capitol Hill where I thought I could make a change, to save those people, to create a world that you yourself are describing." He grabbed a peanut and looked closely at it, admiring it as if holding the secret to life. "It's not possible. You talk about a complex system of nonsense controlling the world. That's true. But it's not what you think. What it actually is, is the obscurity called bureaucracy and the American Justice system." He flicked the peanut at Kennedy, plunking him in the side of the temple. Kennedy flinched and his face reddened. "I'm anti-war, John. My father was shot in the back of his head by a German. I hate war. But the direction you're wanting to take the world is impossible and unprofitable. You want any idea of how I see a slow fix? Orwell. 1984. My favorite novel. A society that is quiet, systematic, trackable, and in place. If it takes a little warring here and there to begin, then ultimately and eventually war will be a thing of the past. It's a grueling, steady climb that will see many dead. In the end, it will all be worthwhile. That's what I believe."

"What you are describing is exactly what Khruschev practices. If you want all that, move to the land of the red. Leave us here if you dislike the current system. I will not send my people to die over your conspiratorial scheme. Fight with your own feet on the ground."

Elder drew a breath. "Many civilians will look back on these years, and the few years to come, and believe this silent revolution to be the greatest social adjustment in human history. And I want to be remembered for being one of those Founding Fathers. So, whatever you plan on doing to prevent me from getting into those textbooks, don't do it. That's my statement."

"I will not be threatened, nor will I conceal the truth from the people of America. They deserve to know the oppression that is coming to them, and they will know whom to fight and how."

Elder shook his head and smiled. "There is so much you don't know. What's in front of you and next to you, you may be able to comprehend. But above you and below, you can't stop it."

Kennedy cocked his head, slightly confused. "I don't think I'll have to. From what I hear and see, you're imploding yourselves."

Elder slammed his hand on the table, making the bowl of snacks jump out of place. "*Walk. Away.* Best advice we can give to a smartass like you."

Kennedy cleared his throat. "I am the President of the United States of America. And I will not allow a brother in politics to break me down. I'm obligated now to tell *my* truth." Kennedy leaned forward and lowered his voice to almost a whisper. "My advice is never become friends with a politician. He will break your heart."

Elder laughed and his voice was intense, almost hissing through his teeth. "Here's how I'm going to leave you, Mr. President; an old story my mother once began telling after my father never came home. Picture a temple. A place of prayer. One that only few divine priests have access to, serving and devoting their entire lives to their god. It is sacred. Within the temple, lies a mystical veil; a portal shrouded in a dense mist. It has existed there for all eternity, as far as the priests are aware. It never changes, moves, or does anything that might intrigue one to enter it. It's to be left alone. On our side of the veil, the real world. On the other, a mystery. One day, a priest, as young and curious as you, is told to stay away and believe the dangers on the other side, just as every priest before him. There is no good reason to look into their god's business. But he does not listen. Ignorantly, he steps into the mist and is immediately paralyzed in fear. He sees demons and spirits flying about, hears screaming in his ears. His terrified howls echoed throughout the temple, lasting long seconds before he was engulfed and went missing from the world. The portal took him because he underestimated it. And now he's gone. The other priests in the temple say his screams were so vile and blood curdling, he must have seen the devil himself. They shake their heads as they can only warn others against entering the misty unknown." Elder stood up, shook the salt from his coat. "This is a fight you have no chance to win. Without choice, you go along. With conscience, you surrender. Don't step any closer to the veil than you have already."

"Shadow governments like yours have fallen before," said Kennedy, standing with Elder now. It was a showdown without guns, but words that weighed a ton. "Whatever you all are, will be next."

Elder outstretched his hand, looking to shake the President's. "They've fallen *because* of us." They shook, and Elder excused himself to the bathroom in the next cabin.

Kennedy sat down. His Secretary of State, Dean Rusk, came from the cabin Elder had entered.

"Mr. President?" Rusk said.

Kennedy waved his hand through the air then sighed, looking out the window at the darkening sky. He couldn't discuss much of what was said to anyone. He knew Rusk was on his side, but the matters at hand were too sensitive to relay to anyone else.

"Are you okay, Mr. President?"

Kennedy thought for a moment. The situation was worse than he originally thought. To move forward with his plans was to endanger himself and even worse, his family or unknowing citizens. He was fighting Godzilla with a knife and one arm behind his back. As positive as he was trying to be, Kennedy knew more people needed knives to fight this monster. Many more. Almost everyone in the world.

"Yes, Dean," said Kennedy. "We'll all be alright. Someday."

Part 5

<u>Atop the Mortal Throne</u>

Fall 1963
Dallas, Texas

HE CHECKED HIS WATCH FOR THE TENTH TIME IN TEN MINUTES. Both hands hovered over the twelve, the small ticker doing its job and hustling around the face of the clock. Every tick like a metronome, controlling the rhythm of his beating heart and jumping nerves. Truthfully, he was mostly calm. He had been trained for this. But even someone trained in this field of expertise to the lengths he has been, should be allowed bouts of nervousness before a major world event unfolds at the pull of a trigger.

His name was not one normally given to a baby at birth, but rather to someone that no longer lives within the rest of humankind: Patton. One name; his alias. Named after George S. Patton, the highly regarded and famous war general for the United States Army during World War II. His strategic mind and exceptional leadership traits were among many attributes that resulted in the successful invasion of Sicily and eventually the liberation of Germany from the Nazis. "A dignified and charismatic leader." Hundreds of thousands of men that stood against him and beside him perished.

And today the man codenamed "Patton" would hope to be just as memorable a figure as his inspiration once was.

Though he couldn't remember most of his life up until a few

years back, the thirty-one-year-old Patton was incredibly bright, muscular, and deadly. He had no recollection of a family, any friends, previous schooling, or anything about himself, except for his career within the Central Intelligence Agency. 1,205 days ago. As far as he could remember, this was essentially the day he was born into the world. His job was his life, and he had nothing outside of it. No social life and no memories to give him any sort of personality.

He was aware that he was different, that something about him was wrong. But he never could guide a thought towards any truth about himself prior to the day he awoke in a lavish New York City hotel 1,205 days ago. All that he found in his room were neatly folded and steamed sets of clothing, a few pairs of expensive shoes, and files of paperwork that reminded him of his memory loss.

According to these documents that he read over a hundred times those first seven days in that hotel, he had been on a mission for the Agency in Central America, spying on communists during the Cold War, when a helicopter flew overhead and rained artillery on his small battalion of operators. He was the lone survivor of the six-man spy operation, but a 5.56x45mm bullet had passed through the left side of his forehead and left him unconscious.

The files read that he was pulled out and rescued by the operations backup crew, but the damage would leave him without most of his memory. As he read his file, he touched the side of his head where he had apparently been shot to discover he really did have a raised scar resting above his left eyebrow, running along the side of his head and ending just over his left ear. Surgery saved his life, he read on. They had removed a part of his skull in the process and replaced the fragmented areas with small lead tiles; four of them to be exact.

Looking down at his watch, the largest hand moved slowly

past the five. Enough time for everything to go according to plan. He tapped at the side of his shaved head where the scar was and could feel the difference under his skin where there was nerveless human tissue and metal. He told himself every time he looked at the scar in the mirror that he would become a leader in intelligence and leave any direct combat behind. No more putting himself in the way of communists. And the Agency had wanted the same for him.

This was his twelfth mission since waking up 1,205 days ago. All eleven others were successful. Some were more successful than others, but nonetheless executed to satisfaction. This was his biggest mission by miles. He had done jobs that were similar, but nothing to this degree, with such a high-level person of interest. It was the first time he had any sort of doubt about himself, as well. Not himself, honestly, but the person he was "guiding" as it was called by the Agency. Patton was selected to be the leader of this three-man mission that would certainly change the world in his company's and country's best interest. But his one partner was a detrimental variable and had failed him once before, in April earlier this year, on a test mission. All previous debriefings and "activations" had proven inconsistent with his partner, but Patton's superiors trusted that this *Joe* was still an asset of use.

Patton checked his watch again. Ten minutes after noon. He sat in a darkened room with several bookshelves occupying each wall to his left and right. Alone, he had been sitting on the diminutive stool placed beside a window that looked out onto the curve where Houston Street became Elm Street. He pulled a small notebook from his shirt pocket and flipped to the back page, reading to himself the unusual string of words that would be nonsense to anyone else except to himself and his partner, who had heard and hopefully understood the coding in a brief ten second meeting between the two of them outside the building earlier this morning, and again on a phone call shortly after. Patton read the words, and his partner, codenamed *Lab*, listened and heard. Heard without a choice.

Patton looked out the window again to see the thin line of people along the street, waving miniature flags in their hands, waiting for this pageantry to commence, their patriotism letting loose. Police bikes patrolled around the bend every minute or two. Several photographers were working their way past the curved road to catch the person of interest smiling and waving as he entered the straightaway. Photographs were being taken of the area: the patrons, the metro, the police, etc... Everyone preparing for what they expected to be a lovely day to support their country's leadership.

And it will be a day. A day to remember for a hundred years. A day of change. A day that future generations will reckon 'lovely'.

Patton unzipped a small black bag that concealed a pair of binoculars. He looked deeper into the crowds of people, specifically seeking out every photographer near the street. All he could do at this point was wait for his partner to complete the mission.

The pounding in his head wouldn't stop. Sweat fell like bullets from his forehead as he tried to clear his mind. He'd strain his eyes open then shut them as hard as he could, wishing to stop the ringing in his ears. Grinding his teeth, he tried to wake himself up from this madness. He must have looked like a freak walking down the hall at his place of work. Thankfully, only one person had seen him as he was pacing the top floor and must've thought nothing of him. The parade for the President nearby was going to draw everyone down to the lowest floor or, better yet, outside.

He arrived at his door at the end of the hall. He put his head up against it as his breathing became more aggressive. He knew he had a mission to complete in five minutes, but he didn't know why or how. His mind was clouded with static. Even as he tried to awaken himself from what felt like a dream, his body continued moving forward and he couldn't fight it. The voices in his head echoed the same dozens of words and they couldn't be silenced. Images flashed in his brain that were unclear and confusing, but when he allowed himself to relax and stopped fighting the images, he felt numbed; better, even. Every few seconds his body grew tired of fighting the dream, and he'd lose nearly all control of what he was doing. It was as if he was being transformed into another person that wanted his crummy life. He stood five feet and nine inches, had short dark hair and beady eyes, a slender build, with another man inside him wanting to break free.

"JUST TAKE IT!" He yelled, slamming his hand on the door in front of him. He yelled and slammed some more. "GET OUT OF MY HEAD!"

He took a deep breath and impulsively he looked at the watch on his wrist he never remembered buying. He straightened out, giving him that calming second to rejuvenate his body, allowing the supposed alter-ego to take over.

"Three minutes until mission is initiated," he said in a relaxed tone. He used the key that was slung around his other wrist by a string to open the locked door. He couldn't remember why there was a key tied to his wrist, either. It was all unreal! All of this!

Behind the door was a storeroom. He was on the top floor of the Texas School Book Depository, where he had been working for over a month now. He walked slowly over to the window as his body twitched and his nerves jerked. To his left was a large pile of cardboard boxes that created a sort of wall. To his right, some more boxes and books were stacked head high. To his front, a gun had been placed on a table. It was a black 6.5x52 mm Carcano Model 38 Italian-made rifle; a short rifle with a bolt-action handle discontinued almost two decades ago; "loaded and ready to go", as the voices said to him. He surged and tried fighting his body again, planting his feet and covering his ears, trying to resist the demons pushing him forward and whispering to him. Grunting like a psychopath, in an empty building. This was a dream.

He heard the mechanical growl of motorcycle engines coming from outside, and he clicked back into the numbed state of obedience. With a suddenly straight face, he moved to the window and looked out to see crowds lining the sidewalks. Police cars and bikes were parked and awaiting the parade's Grand Marshal. His eyes swept over the brightly dressed crowds of people, and then the waving flags of red, white, and blue.

He was locked in after that. The devil himself must've murmured it from behind him, just loud enough for him to be affected and repeat the statement out loud. But it gave him the sudden silence he needed to complete this mission and give him solace.

"Pigs of the sty will weep and cry. Mother of Red, feel no dread," he repeated the devil's words. He picked up the rifle and immediately brought the stock to his shoulder, aiming the short-barreled rifle out of the open window on the sixth floor, waiting for his marker to arrive. His mind was quiet, and he could hear nothing except his own breathing, which had calmed completely. The first few vehicles of the motorcade escorting the Grand Marshal turned around the bend from Houston Street onto Elm.

When Lee Harvey Oswald saw his target, he had transformed

into the other man, tapping all the skills he himself lacked but this other man possessed. His finger moved over the trigger as the open-roof Lincoln Continental Limousine straightened out onto Elm Street. The man inside Oswald fired once, twice, a third time, sending the crowds into panic as President John F. Kennedy sprawled out in a heap, leaving the First Lady to howl in the seat next to him. A mass panic on the streets of downtown Dallas ensued, bringing with it the natural chaos that overwhelms mankind when death is placed at its feet.

The man inside Oswald had suddenly fled, and the clouded mind and headaches returned. He dropped the gun behind a few of the cardboard boxes to his left in a poor attempt to hide the weapon, and lurched toward the door as the sweat began streaming over his eyes.

"Shit! Shit, shit, shit, shit!" Oswald had made a mistake. He was sure of it. Mission accomplished, but he wasn't the one to complete it. He felt it inside himself.

He walked out into the hall, ready to return home. But he didn't know why he had to return home, either. He just had to get there. Taking the stairway down, he replayed the mission in his head. He knew he hit him once, in the middle of the back. His first shot. But after that, his composure wavered. The second shot and third shot definitely had missed high and then right. Did he even fire a third time? He was sure of it! He wasn't even close! He surprised himself with the first shot, not believing that he could hit something that far away and moving at the same time.

He heard footsteps echoing from the first floor of the stairwell, freezing him in place momentarily. He pivoted his way quickly to the door nearest him, pushing through it, and finding himself in the lunchroom on the second floor. At the doorway, he observed a handful of his coworkers had congregated. They were all startled for obvious reasons. Oswald took a deep breath, walked casually over to a vending machine, grabbed a bottle of Coca-Cola, and walked through the lunchroom. *"Casual,"* he coached himself. His supervisor, Roy, was talking with a police officer just a dozen feet in front of him. The officer already had his gun clasped in two hands, at his ready. He must've seen Oswald appear from the stairwell, because his first instinct was to raise his gun at him.

The officer barked something toward him, and the lunchroom attendees panicked some more. Hoots and gasps erupted from the crowd. Oswald slowly raised his hands; one open and the other clenching the bottle of soda while gazing at the officer.

"He's an employee, officer," his supervisor, Roy, said. "Put that down, now!"

Oswald slowly lowered his hands after taking a quick sip of his drink. The officer lowered his gun and apologized briefly, bringing his attention back to his conversation with Roy. So much was happening so fast. Needless to say, everyone was on high alert. Oswald continued forward until a woman he recognized cut across his path and stopped.

"The President has been shot!" She said in astonishment.

Oswald cleared his throat and mumbled under his breath, "Not me…"

She mustn't have heard him, because she remained in his path and stared at him, possibly in wonder. Still in disbelief a gun had been pointed at him in front of all these people, Oswald crept around the woman and headed for the exit, avoiding further confrontation with anyone and being able to make it across the lunch hall to the stairs that took him down to the first floor.

He exited the building through the front doors. The cacophony of everything around him was overwhelming, but it was pulling him slowly out of this nightmarish state he'd been in. He felt as if he were finally waking up and thought that all of this was about to be over. He just wanted to get home.

And then he saw him! A bald, muscular man wearing a black tee-shirt that was tucked into the waist of his jeans. He stared at Oswald. He had a large scar on one side of his head. Oswald had seen this man earlier. They had run into each other on the street hours ago, and the bald man said something cryptic to him while gripping Oswald's wrist, and thus began this spiral that made it feel as if he had been drugged. And after that, a man had called the Depository's phone and asked for Oswald, then spat off yet another meaningless string of words. Psychotic blather! This bald man was now standing outside of the County Records building across the street, eyeing Oswald as he made his way towards the bus stop. Seeing that man made Oswald furious. He was the one inside his head! He was the reason all of this was happening! He had to be!

Oswald ripped the key string off his wrist and threw it to the ground. He had a plan. As his mind slowly began to clear, he feared this was no dream, and he knew one sure thing: he had to kill that ugly bald man.

———————————

Patton watched the police cars and officers patrol the streets for twenty minutes. He was standing at a bus stop at Beckley Avenue near Lab's, or Oswald's, house. After meeting eyes with Lab outside the depository, he knew something was wrong. Patton knew Oswald was observed by multiple people as he left the building. Probably by coworkers inside, too. He surely was a suspect that the police were searching for, and it was a relief to Patton. Oswald was a poor shot. Though the first bullet traveled through the mid-section of the target, his other shot missed. The third man had to do the cleanup. He had expected it from the very start and was ready for it. After he saw the first bullet strike, there was a brief pause before the gun above him was fired again. Luckily, their partner was right there to finish the job. Though this was Patton's operation, someone of greater status and prestige was there as their backup. Patton hadn't met this other operative of his ever before, but knew he was placed in the front seat of that '61 Lincoln Continental cab by his peers. A Secret Service Agent. He would complete the mission for Lab, and it didn't surprise Patton one bit that this was the case. That agent was on his own as anticipated, leaving Patton to deal with the failure.

One failed field test for Lab, and now a failed mission. Patton was aware of the deep instability within his partner, and he was upset that he was allowed to come this far on such a large operation. He'd have to do everything necessary to cut ties between Lab and his employers. Lab had to take the fall.

He used his tongue to feel the chalky fake molar resting inside his mouth, feeling the ridges of the artificial tooth that capsuled the certain death inside it. Today was not his day to depart this world. As he waited for his Joe at this rendezvous point, he was going to follow through with *Protocol C*: release the asset.

In initiating this, Patton assured that the cyanide would sleep another day; or until *Protocol D*.

Oswald pulled on a jacket, pushing the pistol into his waistband. Inside his apartment, he felt that he was nearly back to himself. His head was still aching, but his mind was clear. He did something terrible. He thinks he did, at least. The last few hours were a blur to him until the gunshots had shaken him free from whatever mental prison he was in. Now, in better health, he wanted to know why he recognized that bald man and how he was drugged or hypnotized by him.

He began walking down the street toward the bus stop in his neighborhood. He was going to take the northbound ride back to where all the action was, hoping the bald man was still in the area. He took a seat on a vacant bench, waiting for the next bus to take him back to Elm Street. The police sirens hadn't stopped bouncing off the buildings and wailing through the city of Dallas. His foot tapped nervously as he was preparing himself to possibly kill this suspicious man. He felt the cold steel of the weapon in his pants push into his thigh and just prayed the safety was on.

He had no time to react. From behind him, the bald man appeared, wrapping his arm around Oswald's neck to keep him quiet and still. Oswald fought for his life as the chokehold held him down. Close to his ear, the bald man whispered words that were all too familiar to Oswald, and he began to cry, anticipating the forthcoming result.

"Golf, pig, Moscow, November, Japan, roses, three. Mother is cooking dinner, return to Charlie."

Patton released Oswald as he went limp on the bench. He sat in awe as his brain was being ripped apart by psychedelic colors and waves. White turning yellow, then to green, to blue, then the red turning to purple, fading to black. Oswald turned his head slowly around only to see no one there. The person who had been holding him down was gone. What did he look like? Who was that? Why did it matter?

He was calm the moment a patrol car slowly approached him, stopping at the curb in front of him. He stood himself up and felt nauseated. Looking at the cloudless autumn sky, he wasn't sure where he was at the moment. He'd gone foggy again, but he felt free from the dream. He looked around at his surroundings, breathing through his mouth like a confused toddler, wondering where his mother went in the supermarket. He was a lost child.

He approached the passenger side of the patrol car. The window was rolled down and the officer driving began to talk with him.

"Hello, sir," the officer started. "Have you spent any time down by Elm Street today?" The officer seemed on edge.

Oswald with a blank stare said, "I don't believe so."

"You mean you can't remember?" The officer was stern now. "It's not too late in the day, sir—"

"I don't believe so," Oswald repeated.

The fix was in. The officer opened the driver-side door and got out of the vehicle, knowing something was going on with Oswald. He walked around the front of the cab and began reaching for his handcuffs attached to his belt.

"Put your hands behind your head…"

That's all the police officer was able to get out, as Oswald pulled the .38 caliber revolver from his waistband and fired three shots into his chest. The officer crashed to the pavement. Oswald immediately stepped closer and stood over him, staring at the wounded officer, and firing one fatal last shot into the officer's head.

Oswald felt nothing. He was calm, emotionless. His mind was as black as a newborn's. He turned and fled the scene at the corner of Tenth and Patton Avenue.

Later that day, after an altercation and another attempted shooting at an officer inside the Texas Theatre, Oswald was arrested and charged with the murder of Officer J.D. Tippit and President John F. Kennedy. Throughout his interrogation on the matter, he denied every single accusation. He repeatedly claimed during the process that he was "just a patsy". He came off as a lunatic: deranged, disoriented, and mad. In his background, the investigators discovered that he had lived for a short while in the Soviet Union, and had assumed the rivaling political conflicts had much to do with the assassination.

He was to face trial two days later.

When that day came, Agent Patton was hidden in a lake of people and watched as Lab was being transported to an armored vehicle outside the Dallas Police Headquarters. It was to bring him to his trial. Before he reached the vehicle, Lab was shot in the abdomen by Jack Ruby, local club owner. Patton did not flinch as the crowd erupted. Instead, he closed his eyes and was glad his job had been done for him by another madman; a mad, unforeseen, uncontrollable variable. Jack Ruby.

The past forty-eight hours that Oswald had sat in custody had worried Patton about the release of his asset. He banked on the confused man's loose wiring up top to discredit every word that came from his lips. But Patton sat in his hotel room in downtown Dallas worried that someone would believe the sick bastard. So, against his orders, he came here armed to ensure all ties were cut. He believed with his skills and connections he could disappear. If only he had more faith in the Agency's methods and technology, he'd already be enjoying his vacation in Bermuda by now.

"Thank God for Jack Ruby," Patton thought as he calmly picked his way through the horde of nescient bystanders. Ignorant, unaware, and helpless; he is doing them all a favor. The future relies on the present, which relies on the past. Without the past, there is no future. And whatever is to come of humanity, Patton will be a catalyst shaping that future. He is sure of it. Two days ago, a lesson had been taught to the people of the United States. It would always be remembered if this country continued to exist. He had taught them that this *must* be remembered. And

he will live to teach these people another lesson in history…
someday soon.

If you enjoyed the read, don't hesitate to leave a review anywhere on the web!

As an Indie author, reviews are a major way to help get my name out there to more readers! Wherever you can find my book, a review is greatly appreciated!

If you want to find me online or find a different version of this book, just head over to my socials or my personal website provided below!

Website: **alih64.square.site**
Author Instagram: **@stephenrtracy64**
Series Instagram: **@anotherlessoninhistory**
X: **@StephenRTracy64**
Facebook: **Stephen R. Tracy**